I0725623

Heart

Diamondsong

A Concerto in Ten Parts

Part 03:
Heart

E.D.E. Bell

Atthis Arts
Detroit, Michigan

Ðiamondsong
Part 03: Heart

Copyright ©2019 by E.D.E. Bell
edebell.com

This is a work of fiction.
Any resemblance to actual pyrsi, winged or otherwise, is purely coincidental.

Cover Art by M.C. Krauss

Map of Ada-ji by Ulla Thynell

Interior Design by G.C. Bell

Editorial Services by:
Camille Gooderham Campbell
Catherine Jones Payne and Haley Tomaszewski, Quill Pen Editorial
M. Cusack

All rights reserved.

Published by Atthis Arts, LLC
Detroit, Michigan
atthisarts.com

ISBN 978-1-945009-32-7

Library of Congress Control Number: 2018967628

First Edition: Published January 2019

This book is dedicated to Vashti.

Always my heart.

PREFACE

My notes for this preface said only one thing, and that was to offer extra thanks to Trowby Brockman and to explain what an important part of this process she has been.

So it is with a deeply heavy heart that I now realize she will never see that note I planned to write, because she passed away on 19 November 2018, days before she was set to proofread this volume. It was unexpected, from an illness that had been diagnosed just 20 days earlier.

I will still write the note.

Trowby volunteered to proofread *The Banished Craft* in early 2015, saying that she believed in my writing. Her words meant a lot, as did her help. As the trilogy continued, she proofread each piece, always encouraging me with how much she enjoyed it and how it made her think. She also pointed out errors. It became a joke between us how I was improving in my writing, no longer needing her to save me from "it peaked my interest" but moving on to more subtle flaws and opportunities. And she thought it was funny when, later, I worked in "piqued" just for her.

She was so excited when she saw General Trow in *The Fettered Flame*, described as having a *snout over his teeth*. Excited enough that I wished I had done more with it! I at least made sure that Trow showed his own strength in *The Scattered Bond*, enough to make Zee doubt his allegiance. I apologized to Trowby for him not being a good guy or having a larger role, and Trowby said, no, she loved him and saw that he had a sense of ethics. She said she was so excited to have a dragon named after her.

And then in *Escape*, she flagged an awkwardly worded moment that could have reflected poorly on Dime's hygiene, resulting in the revised text: *to wash in the water or relieve herself.*

The last book of mine Trowby read was *Capture*, where she asked me why a guard would gurgle, and embarrassed, I had to write back, I don't know—that's pretty weird. And then I went and changed it! She told me that she loved *Capture* and was even more excited for the series to continue. She said she was excited to stay a part of it, that she felt she really was contributing. I replied that she always contributed. Not long after, she was diagnosed. I didn't know this; I simply learned she was gone.

From talking to her friend, I learned that she chose her own way of leaving. She asked that medical devices be removed, instead opting to be as she was, surrounded by those she loved. "She wanted to go on her terms," the friend told me. The tagline for *Capture* was: *On my terms* and its primary theme was doing what you hadn't wanted to do, but doing it on your terms. I will always think of Trowby when I see those words.

And now I present to you that next installment that Trowby was excited to read: *Heart*. I hope you enjoy it.

As always, a book like this takes a team to do right. And so, my extensive gratitude to Catherine Jones Payne, Camille Gooderham Campbell, Megan Cusack, Haley Tomaszewski, Sasha Kasoff Moore, Laura Johnson, and Deborah Reilly.

And here's the part where I was going to tell Trowby how much she meant to me. Instead, I will tell you. Trowby was a pure light in this world. A positive soul who reached out to help others. She was clever, kind, and funny. And she saved my books from some goofy stuff, because let's face it, there's enough of that already.

Remember, don't wait to tell people what they mean to you. Even if it was meant to be a surprise.

Maybe go talk to someone today: someone who has meant something to you. Show them your heart.

My love to you,

Emily.

January 2019

The World of Ada-ji

The Ja-lal: A humanoid species, dwelling in the foothills and plains of Ada-ji, characterized by broad advancements in construction, invention, and health. The Fo-ror call them brutes.

The Fo-ror: A winged humanoid species, dwelling in the forests of Ada-ji, characterized by their natural living and the use of magical powers, known as valence. The Ja-lal call them fairies.

The Ja-lal and Fo-ror are similar in form, with gray skin, but differences between them in composition and culture. Pyr is singular for a Ja-lal or Fo-ror and pyrsi is plural.

The pyrsi of Ada-ji hold many **gender identities**. While this doesn't clarify all aspects of gender, it is polite to introduce oneself with a prefix, indicating the appropriate pronouns:

- **Fe'** indicates a set of feminine identities, using the pronouns she/her/her(s).
- **Ma'** indicates a set of masculine identities, using the pronouns he/him/his.
- **Ji'** indicates a set of spectrum identities, using the pronouns ve/ver/vis.

When gender is unknown, it is polite to refer to a pyr with xe/xem/xyr(s). Any group of pyrsi (plural) would be referred to with they/them/their(s).

A pyr may be generically referred to as **Burge**, short for the more formal Burgess, often for purposes of polite address or getting a stranger's attention. This is similar to the use of Sir or Ma'am on Earth. For those who hold social prejudice based on class, the term implies some sense of status or honor.

Ja-lal and Fo-ror may live up to 50 cycles. Their lives are divided into defined **epochs**, aligning with societal expectations:

Aoch	Age 0-9	Characterized by upbringing, education, and exploration
Bakh	Age 10-19	Centered on building family, performing and completing apprenticeships, and finalizing life plans
Gamh	Age 20-29	Fully immersed in their specialty or role, contributing full-time to society
Dorh	Age 30-39	Respected in leadership and/or advisory roles; it is normal to take some time for self
Eroh	Age 40+	Expected to retire and engage in craft or occasional consulting, through the **life expectancy of around 50 cycles**.

Expectations differ for each culture. For example, while a Ja-lal must develop xyr profession into a career, a Fo-ror's profession and rank are set based on xyr social class and other historical and cultural factors.

A **cycle** on Ada-ji is perhaps up to four times the length of an Earth year. So, our main character, at age 20.5 cycles, has lived more than 80 Earth years but, in relation to her life span, could be considered at the **maturity of her early forties** on Earth.

Each **turn** on Ada-ji, a period of day and then night, is **significantly longer than an Earth day**. As such, pyrsi do not sleep according to light or dark, but instead based on their own needs, lifestyle, profession, and schedule.

The Ja-lal measure time by the periodic sounding of bells; they refer to the resultant time periods with the same term. The Fo-ror are less rigid about time-keeping and refer to the equivalent time period as a span. Each **bell**, or **span**, consists of more than two Earth hours.

Smaller amounts of time are referred to by both cultures as **takes**, which can be thought of as about ten Earth minutes.

In Earth terms, it has been almost four weeks since the beginning of our tale.

The Ja-lal and Fo-ror live on separate sides of the Great Cliff. They have not interacted since the ***Great War***, an event most noted for being the **end of the Violence** on Ada-ji.

Synopsis to Here

Fe'Diamond, known as Dime, had just left her career working for the Circles, the government of the Ja-lal. Suddenly, three hooded figures burst into her home with ropes, demanding to take her away. Without any understanding of why this had occurred, Dime and her spouse, Dayn, ran to escape them.

The intruders were revealed to be Fo-ror, commonly known as fairies. These fairies, unseen since the conclusion of the Great War, were feared and loathed by the Ja-lal, who were taught that any contact would cause the Violence to return. The fairies were said to employ a magical power known as valence, but Dime had thought this a myth—perhaps that even the fairies themselves were a myth—until she saw both herself.

Dime escaped from the city and, finally evading the fairies' continued pursuit, she was rescued by a large animal species known as newts. Living amongst them, she befriended a young newt she called Juni. It became apparent to her that the Fo-ror had driven the newts from their original home, keeping them away from Fo-ror civilization with large barriers of rope netting. She was brought back to Sol's Reach by a fe'pyr familiar with fairies, Ella. Together they headed for Dime's home in the large Ja-lal city of Lodon, but found it stirred up by a fringe political group named Sol's Pillars. Instead, they traveled to Ella's home on the edge of the old woods, where Ella broke the news that, for reasons yet unknown, Dime was biologically a Fo-ror—one whose wings had been removed.

After recovering from her injuries, Dime traveled to the forest land of the fairies, the Heartland, to learn more about her past. There, in the city, Pito, she found that her old colleague and former flame, Agent Rock, had gone to find her, landing herself in Fo-ror prison, a concept unfamiliar to the Ja-lal. After they'd spent some time catching up in their cells, Rock helped Dime escape, with Dime promising to return to assist Rock.

Dime met with the High Seat, Ferala, who confessed that she was part of an old scheme to avenge the horrors of a disease called the curse, which the Fo-ror blamed on the Ja-lal. This scheme, designed by now Third Seat Neimano, was named Project Diamondsong. Neimano's plan was to remove the wings from Fo-ror newborns, place them in positions of potential influence amongst the Ja-lal, and then allow them to grow up before activating their loyalties as Fo-ror spies.

Dime has just arrived outside her home city of Lodon, where, with Neimano's cold gaze fixed in her mind and mobs of Sol's Pillars surrounding the city's gates, she feels an urgency to return to and protect her family.

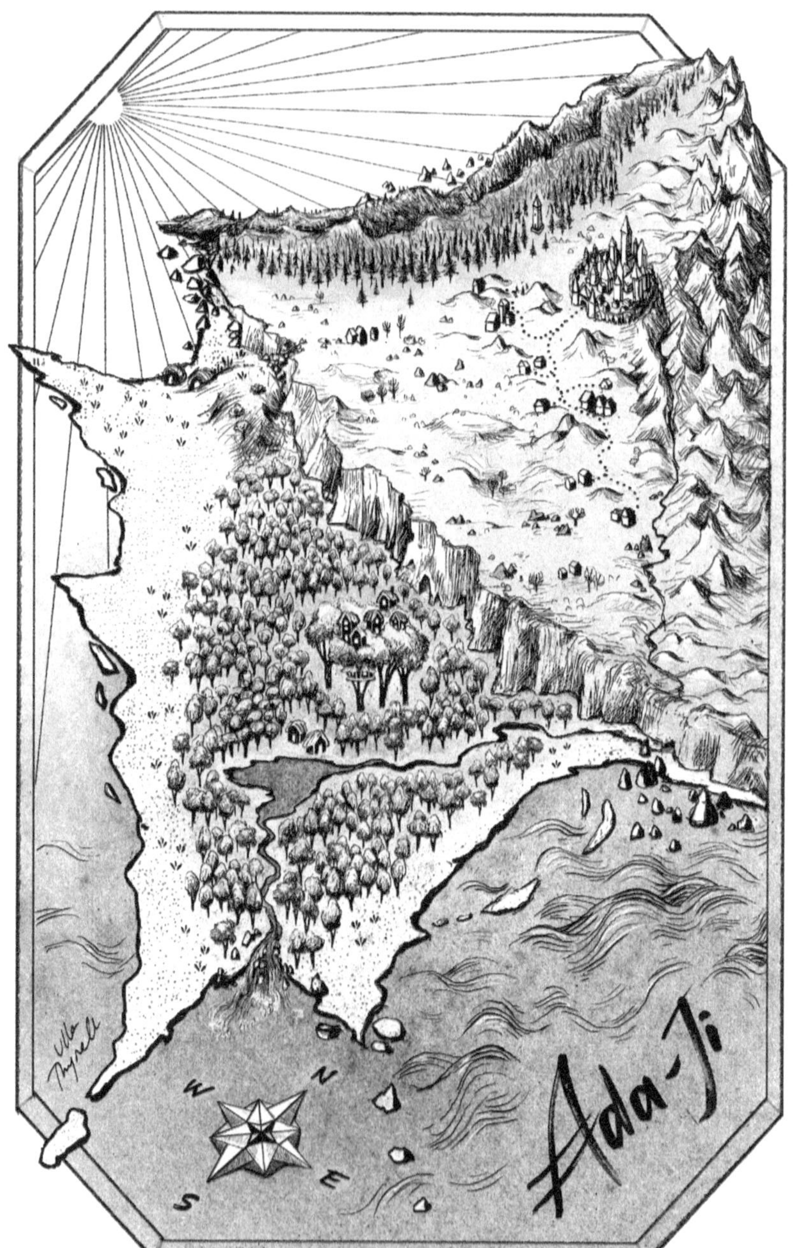

Ada-Ji
W
N
E
S

Heart

This way, that way
I do not know what to do: I am of two minds

—Psappho, recovered fragment, c600 BCE

Act 1

HOME

There is a specific reaction to seeing a place one views as xyr home, especially if that home has changed. Dime stared at Lodon's distant towers, conflicted between the comfort of their sight—of believing her family was there, waiting—and a mix of new, dissonant feelings, of being on the outside, far away, of not knowing how much of the city's welcome had been taken from her.

Now aware that biological Ja-lal did not see in the dark as well as she did, Dime was pleased to see Sol setting as she approached Lodon's walls. She took a long stride to marvel at the colors and shadows of Sol's light lowering over the mountains and towers of her home. Oddly, she found herself wishing Ferala were here to see it.

The bells echoed out from the towers and Dime felt soothed by the familiar sound. It was hard to consider how much had transpired since the last bells she'd heard, as she was racing away from Lodon in a toothcar, her mind spinning and heart pumping and Neimano's guards in her pursuit. She peered toward the Great Gates, almost glowing with the sharp reflection of the waning light.

While the throngs of Sol's Pillars surrounding the Great Gates were not as organized or as energetic as the last time she'd seen them, they appeared to have grown in size. She wasn't sure what they even thought they were doing—whether they were just rallying, or if they had a specific mission, like watching for fairies. Maybe they were even watching for her.

It had been, she considered it, more than seven long turns since the fairies had intruded into Lodon. Though she couldn't be sure, having been outside the city this whole time, she didn't think the fairies had returned. She glared ahead at the mob lining the entrance to the city, blocking its main entrance.

How long are they willing to keep this up?

Dime was unsure how long one invasion could be used to fuel their momentum. And what was the next step? Did they have a goal? Now that they had broken into plain sight, could they put their banners away and dissipate back into normal life? Would they?

They at least had that choice. Dime didn't know what her next step was either, but she didn't have the option to just return to her life. As it appeared, she couldn't even enter the city.

She'd traveled to the Heartland looking for answers. In some sense, she'd got what she needed. She knew why the Seats had placed her with the Ja-lal and what had been the catalyst for their trying to force her away.

Now that Dime no longer served her purpose of ascension to Light's Circle, Neimano had ordered her brought back. Based only on Ferala's story, Dime would've thought Neimano intended to convince her to return to the IC, to operate as a witting agent for the Fo-ror. But seeing Neimano's enthusiasm for the cages, the way he'd treated her as Ja-lal, she believed he'd meant to imprison her and learn what she knew from her cycles of internal IC exposure. She would satisfy her duty, as he saw it, another way. But as Dime saw it, duty required some level of ethical concurrence.

Then what duty did she have? High Seat Ferala had helped her escape, yet he'd hinted that he could not see the current truce between Fo-ror and Ja-lal continuing much longer.

Dime didn't know whether he thought it was Neimano's intrusion into Lodon that would open the gates to War, or any new actions the Third Seat intended, or just a general sense that the two societies were discovering each other, one incident at a time. There was a reason undiscovery wasn't a word, one of her teachers used to say.

What Ferala hadn't said, but Dime surmised, was that knowing the precarity of the situation was why both governments fought so hard to keep information contained. Even when that meant hiding the truth. Dime stared across at the mob.

She knew, as Ferala did, that after generations of mutually-fostered ill will, there was too much static charge built into that relationship for it to settle on an easy peace. Without intervention, a return of the Great War was possible. Likely, even. Had Ferala released her in hopes she could try and stay the conflict?

How could one pyr prevent a War?

Dime felt powerless. Alone. She pondered this as the shadows raced over the hills, and the last daylight disappeared.

Her priority was to find her family. While she'd vowed again and again not to hide or live her life in hiding, she no longer trusted for her family's safety. She didn't know if Sol's Pillars were dangerous or just full of hot air. Perhaps both. But she'd seen Neimano's cold eyes, felt his gaze upon her. Like many lines recently, the Violence no longer felt like a hard line to her, and Neimano had crossed it before.

Would he—it was hard to think it, but she must—would he *harm* her children in the interest of the Fo-ror? She didn't know. Would he justify locking them in crystal cages to draw Dime back? For the "safety" of the Fo-ror? Yes. He would.

Just the idea was the Violence. Her stomach churned, and she could not shake the mental images of her children behind those cold metal bars, though she urged herself to blink them away. He would not get near her children.

So that was the easy choice: to find her family and move them away until the situation had settled. She would go in, find her family, and together, they'd get out.

The harder question was the step after that. One version of this story had her leaving for the hills and living among mountain folk or outlaws, who avoided authority and wouldn't give her away. Or building a home near Ella in the old woods and hiding there. Either might render a long life of worry, even if normalcy settled back into both lands.

No, Dime reminded herself, that would not happen. Ferala didn't think it would happen, and she agreed with him. Pyrsi in Lodon had seen fairies and the Circles couldn't tell them they hadn't. And Dime had showed herself to the gardener in Pito; she couldn't remember his name. Who would he tell? "I met a Ja-lal." It could start there.

This cart was sliding down the tunnel, as Da-da would say. The options spinning in her mind, she tried to focus. She would see what she could learn while in the city. She would get her family out. And then she could consider what her role in this was. What she could even do.

It had been a long walk across Sol's Reach, over most of the daylight. And, she vowed, she was not doing that again without a *toothcar*. That decision was made too.

Her next decision was whether to walk through the crowds of Sol's Pillars gathered outside, taking a gamble on what would happen if they recognized her. While the bravado of her declaration never to hide again still resonated, she'd feel much better taking risks once her children were safely away.

The Sol's Pillars looked a mess, gathered around. Some still tried to form jagged lines and shake their banners. Others sat on blankets, appearing to relax—some were even having a picnic—and one perhaps less-devoted follower had fashioned a kite from the *Caller* and was running in a wide arc, gliding the flapping paper through the evening light.

Their continued expansion was irritating for several reasons, primarily that this most divisive of factions was the one that pyrsi had run to after the Fo-ror intrusion. Not to friends and family. Not to Ador's Free Winds, a group dedicated to challenging the way Lodon operated, nor to any of the specialized political clubs that morphed in and out of favor. Not even to the Circles. No, they'd run to the voices who fostered discontent, and, she now understood, used ignorance and fear about the fairies to fuel it. Dime glared at the amassed crowd.

She didn't see a way to sneak past them; no one could approach Lodon covered or concealed, even before. And Ella had said it was common knowledge that Dime was the one who had been attacked and gone missing—surely enough pyrsi in her tower had seen her and spread word of her build and tattoos. Whatever they thought of her, she'd never pass by without pyrsi questioning her or following her throughout the city.

Dime wasn't hanging under a toothcar again, or running on loose stones, or falling over cliffs, or doing anything that would risk injury. She watched, as some seemed to arrive while others left their ranks. Leaving for home or their jobs, she presumed, with the passing of the bells and the arrival of night. And others, now available, arriving to ensure a continued presence.

She set her bag on the ground with a grumble.

Ja-lal loved tattoos, and took especial care with selecting those to adorn their faces. Tattoos were identity, they were art, they grew and faded with age like a metaphor for life itself. Every Ja-lal created xyr own unique identity, recognizable from the rest. Yet, Dime now understood, they made it really easy to find a pyr who wasn't looking to be found.

The art stick with which Ella had previously given her a false hemsa had been shoved in a lower pocket with a fair amount of disdain. Now, getting it out along with a mirror and wishing she had one of those fairy glow lights, she leaned against a boulder and shook her head.

Visualizing the hubbub at the gates, she thought it might work. Once. *Once!* She was not doing this again. But she just wasn't ready yet for pyrsi to know she was here. And, from its previous use, she knew this pigment washed off.

Squinting into the little mirror, she drew a prominent symbol of Sol on her left cheek and decorated over her beautiful vines with common, unmemorable markings. Though irritated by the whole enterprise, she figured she'd better do it right, so she drew on a few extra vines as well.

Walking toward the outer reaches of the gathering, she worked herself in amongst the crowd. A few pyrsi turned her way, peering at her markings. Some pointed and whispered to each other. As the whispers tore through the crowd, some of the looks of confusion turned to disgust—or even fear. If she was going to go through with it, it had to be now.

With a loud whistle, she hopped out amongst the staring pyrsi. "Hey, look at me! I'm Agent Dime, back from the fairies!" She adopted a mock march, swinging her arms as she moved forward. "The vines are on my face!" She pointed with the art stick, still in her hand.

"The fairies are our friends!" Around her, pyrsi had quieted. Worried that her ruse was failing, she bellowed with forced laughter and said the first thing that came to mind. "I'm here to *take Ja-lal children away!*"

"Ha!" a pyr shouted out. "That's what I said! That traitor went with the fairies!" Pyrsi all around laughed and roared their insults.

"I still think they *killed* her," another called out, raising an equal murmur of assent, pierced with gasps at the harsh language. "And they'll come back for us!"

Around her, the arguments grew as Dime marched forward, shouting indistinct cheers and staying as far away as she could from anyone with a lamp.

She zig-zagged back and forth through the crowd, smacking offered hands and working her way up toward the front. "Huzzah!" she yelled, spinning and pumping her arms into the air. Roaring, they all tried to imitate her. Lost among the swirl of protestors, she slipped in through the gates, as the Circles toll-takers and stressed-looking Enforcement officers futilely tried to calm everyone down.

As soon as she could, Dime ran from the main road, away from the larger structures, and entered the first public bath that she found, a small unit with cracked tiles and grimy windows. Locking the door and stripping off her tunic, she soaped her face, pumped the small chest-level basin full of water, and scrubbed until every bit of the false markings had washed away, leaving her vine tattoos clear across her scalp.

Collapsing against the wall with the broken tile floor beneath her, she wrapped her hands around her stomach. She felt sick for these buffoons, sick to have fueled it, and sick now knowing that her first entrance to this city had been in Neimano's arms, flying overtop its walls. Her home, sure. Dropped here as a baby, meant to betray everyone she had ever known. That knowledge had *hurt* her, she acknowledged. Another scar, now.

She shouldn't have played along back there, but she'd just wanted to get through them without being followed. They'd seen her; they'd noticed her vines. Their initial expressions had been revolted, concerned. *"What am I supposed to do?"* she shouted to the dark walls of the bathhouse, disgusted.

Dime dried off and got dressed. As she left the little room, glad to see no one was waiting to use it, she tossed the art stick down, not watching to see where it clattered among the old tiles.

It was a long walk to her tower, but she'd made it this far without a car and she could survive it another couple of bells. Traversing the shadowy alleys of Lodon, Dime kept her distance from the lamps and avoided the popular areas of the city. In most places, it looked like the city she knew, the one she had left. She tried to quell the trembling in her fingers, rubbing one hand against the other, as she made her way upcity.

The first pyr to recognize her was a tower employee. Xe had a mishmash of chunky tattoos, and a plain working suit; Dime had seen xem around. She didn't remember xyr name, but xe remembered hers.

"Dime, thank Sol, you're alive." Xe paused, as if at a loss for what to say. Dime, her earlier ruse still knotted in her stomach, wanted to make up for it. With anything.

"I am. I think we'd agree—best to keep it quiet for now. Instead, tell pyrsi this: fairies are real and they're a lot like us. Some good ones, some less good ones."

"That does fit us here," xe said with a nervous laugh, as xyr eyes dimmed with unease.

"They didn't take me," she continued, her hand moving over her heart. "I got away. Things might change. I don't know. Just . . . tell everyone the Violence is not the solution and we must all work to prevent it. What you've been told about the fairies is . . . a lie. Ok?" Wincing, she realized she'd basically just accused the Circles of the Violence, twice. Once in the suggestion they'd propose it, and twice in the suggestion that they'd lied.

It was clear to Dime that events, including her return, hadn't fully caught up to the worker yet. Maybe best to move on. "I'll be out of here soon. It would help me out if you could raise the bucketpull for me. Without calling for the operators, I mean. I've got to get up to my place, and the fewer pyrsi I run into, the better . . . for all of us? Don't you agree?"

"Yes . . . I think so," xe murmured, setting down a bucket and rag and moving over toward the crank. Xe said nothing else to Dime, and Dime, not used to feeling like an outsider in her own home, got quickly into the bucket and closed the latch.

It was a rough trip up with only one operator; this reminded Dime why, unless she was with Tum, she always took the stairs. However, no one gave the wooden bucket a look as it notched up through the crowded lower floors of the tower. Dime hopped out at the first hub and, rather than risking her luck with a second helper, she zipped over to the stairs and didn't wait to see if anyone had seen her.

In between bells, pyrsi weren't as much coming and going, especially here on the residential floors. A few pyrsi had their eyes buried in the *Caller*, and one pyr snored in a reclined seat. Dime hurried up the stairs, her legs burning; she hadn't been on stairs for so long!

Dime marveled, as she climbed the curved staircase, at her new reaction to the smell of brew in the tower hubs. Previously it had been one of her favorite smells of home and welcome, but after Ella's expertly roasted beans, it just smelled bitter. She knew that big things in her life had changed—but these little things—they almost shocked her more.

She was glad to see no one posted outside her home, no activists or fairies or anything else. Her hand against the door, she peered through the widening crack, not wanting to knock but also hoping not to startle her family inside.

Still ungreeted, she walked into the living area and lit the main lamp. It was clear no one was living here now, and the emptiness hit her like a small rush of wind. She'd taken one step after another, each one revealing a new journey she'd have to make without her family, and here she was again. Thinking she might see them, and then not. Well. She'd made it this far, and she'd keep going from here. She breathed in.

The home hadn't been emptied, but anything necessary or precious to Dayn or the kids was gone. This was a relief; if they'd been removed under duress, they wouldn't have taken their favorite books, and Dayn wouldn't have carefully double-latched all the windows.

While she was glad they'd had the caution to leave, she wasn't sure where they would have gone. In fact, that might be the point.

Dayn was smart. He'd have a way to find her.

The crate with the rest of the items from her office was still sitting on the table. Ignoring it, she decided to go get that drink. Certainly, Dayn wouldn't have taken all the ferm, not when he knew Dime would come here to find him.

She was glad there wasn't a note for her in the ferm cabinet—that would be too much—but, yes, he'd left one bottle of an herbal right in the middle, next to a low glass. Since he'd shut off the water chiller, it made sense to leave something that was fine at natural temperature. She chuckled, pouring herself a little.

Flopping down onto the cushions of the bench, she swirled the greenish ferm around in the bottom of the glass.

I'm back, she thought. *Story's over.*

It was impossible to convince herself that was true. Perhaps she should have been more cautious, sitting in her own home with a tower full of pyrsi who could have seen her arrive. For a take or two, she just stopped worrying about it. She was so tired of running, and hiding, and sneaking. And he'd left a good herbal—

Dime knew she'd better figure out what she wanted to do and get to it.

Leaning over to the game drawer, she was amused to see the kids had taken their favorite items, including Dime's large bag of dice. She did have a stack of older dice bags, and she took a nice soft one so Ador's gift would have a safer home in her pocket. She grabbed a couple of the better sets of cards, grumbling how no one else appreciated the really good decks.

She walked back into her sleeping area. Dayn had arranged the pillows in the form of a smiley face, so they must not have gone somewhere too uncomfortable. She set her hand on one and smiled.

Dime could only carry so much on her back, but she found comfort in grabbing a couple of her own outfits, her best skin lotion, and her father's heirloom bracelets. Looking around the house for anything else she wanted to use or keep safe—except books, which she wasn't going to drum around in a backpack—she decided she'd pressed her luck here long enough.

With still no clues where her family had gone, she'd check on her father; either they were staying with him or he'd have some idea where they went.

Back in the living area, she stood at the wide window and drank in one long view of Lodon's towers in the diffused light of the skystones. It was hard to know she couldn't stay. Not tonight.

She clicked off the lamp, as a sinking feeling told her she'd never stay here again. She hoped that wasn't true.

As she passed the tall hallway window, she imagined for a moment what it would be like to perch on its edge and fly off into the sky, deeply-hued wings flapping behind her. She'd never know.

Heavy with these thoughts, Dime managed to make it out of the tower without anyone paying attention to her, though she supposed the bulky backpack made her look like she was making deliveries. She walked down the streets, staying near the walls and avoiding eye contact. Her stomach gurgled, knowing it was only a matter of time until someone recognized her. At least someone who wanted to make an issue of it.

And it was only a matter of time before one of the Sol's Pillars questioned her charade. Or even someone with a little sense, hearing the story. Once rumors started that she was back, all eyes would be out for her.

Da-da lived quite a way downcity, but Dime kept to the shadows and stayed out of view. The pyrsi in his lobby were so engaged in a card game they didn't give her a look as she darted into the stairwell. Moving to the third floor, she walked down a hallway and rapped at the door.

It was interesting to notice how well she blended in amongst the Ja-lal, just as she had for a lifetime. Sure, someone would eventually recognize her or her markings, but it was upsetting how much she stood out in Pito and how little she stood out here. There was an irony in that, one she supposed Neimano had not considered.

Normally, her father would just shout "I'm here," but he must have recognized her knock. Beaming, he swung the door open and wrapped his huge, sturdy arms around her. Dime edged past him, working to move inside.

"Diamond," he wheezed. "You're safe. That nice fe'pyr, she said so, but just I had to see you to know! Now, get in here." Gorg closed the door behind them, and for the first time since this all began, Dime felt completely and totally safe.

Setting her backpack at the wall, she rushed again into her father's arms, and all the worries and stress and tension of the last long turns rushed out. He rocked her back and forth as they stood, singing under his breath.

"Squash Blossom, it's so good to see you."

"Da-da," Dime murmured, joy surging through her. He hadn't called her that in a long time.

She was glad to see he looked well. "Has anyone bothered you here, Da-da?" Dime felt sick at the idea of anyone harassing her father; she already knew Dayn would have tried to get him to go with them, and he'd probably refused.

"Only the Dorh on the fourth floor," he whispered. "New to tower living, let's say. But we've got it straightened out now." He raised his voice back to normal tones. "Here, Blossom, sit down and I'll make you some tea."

A hot tea did sound nice. She remembered Tikinal bringing Ferala a whole new cup every time his sat a touch. Maybe she didn't need to tell Da-da yet that she'd met the High Seat. Or that there *was* a High Seat. One thing at a time.

"You must have heard, Da-da," she said, watching his reaction with concern.

She did not expect him to start bellowing a tune.

> *An adventure blows this way on the wind*
> *An adventure rides on the wind*
> *Will you shelter from the gale?*
> *Or will you fly with it?*

"Da-da," Dime murmured, knowing he must have been worried. Nothing seemed to shake the ma'pyr's spirits.

"Let me get you that tea," he said, shuffling off through the door.

Dime rested back in a squishy old chair that had always been her favorite. The living area was much how it always had been. Gorg's furnishings were almost all ones he'd made himself out of scrap he'd been offered and his own unique handywork.

Her father wasn't an artist by any stretch, but he had an eye for practicality that she'd always admired. The chairs sat just right and the tables weren't too high or too low. Every piece had an attached shelf or two—little side tables to hold a bowl of crisp sticks or a small cup of water—and every seat had an attached foot bar for resting feet.

He'd made Tum her very own chair, one built specially for a pyr without legs. It had bars for arms and a sloped base, so she could lean back and enjoy conversation or a meal with the others. Her gaze fixed on the chair, she thought again how much she missed Tum. She thought again of Luja and Dayn. It hadn't been so terribly long, but the inability to console them—to show that she was fine—weighed on her more than she'd allowed herself to admit. Again, she wondered if he knew where they'd gone. If he did, he'd tell her.

Gorg walked back into the room, placing a steaming mug onto the rest beside her chair. "You always take my best chair."

Dime grinned. "But you have it the rest of the time."

In that moment of talking about chairs, Dime finally detected a shadow in her father's eyes. Something he wasn't telling her, hidden behind the unconcealed relief at seeing her again. He saw her staring at him and he offered a smile.

"They're all fine, Blossom. Tough as a chisel, that lot."

Dime was glad to hear it.

"I'm not supposed to say anything," he cautioned. "I've got something for you later."

That made sense. Dayn would have known she'd try here. Not wanting Gorg to be taken advantage of, he'd probably left some clue, but otherwise told Gorg not to talk to anyone about Dime. Which Gorg had taken so seriously, he was now hesitant to talk to Dime herself. She almost laughed.

"Of course, Da-da. I'm glad you're all well. I know . . . I know this has been a lot. I'm sorry about all of it. What you've been through."

"Diamond, I . . . I'm so proud of you." He waved a hand. "No, don't tell me about your career again; you'll work that out. You. Your family. Your smile. Your . . . energy." Gorg's eyes flitted sideways.

As comfortable as Dime felt here, there was an intensity in the air, a sense of unrest. She could have told her father not to worry, but it affected her too; it had since the first moment the fairies had burst through her door.

Even today, rather than just visit with her father, she was troubled by lingering questions in the back of her mind. About her birth. What he might have seen or known. She'd always assumed he'd told her anything he knew, but maybe there was more. Looking up into his eyes, she didn't know if she was seeing her father's insecurities, or if he was reflecting her own.

She couldn't do this over and over. She couldn't fret, and stress, and question what each pyr knew or didn't know. Dime let it all go. She'd rather be here, with her father, and enjoy his company.

"Da-da, let's sing a song."

Gorg's fleeting look of concern broke into a wide, fatherly grin. "Now, that's my child. Here, I know just the one! How about one of our folk tales?"

Dime had long doubted that her father's songs qualified as folk tales; she was pretty sure he'd made up the whole lot. For the next several takes, she didn't care. She sipped her tea as they sang of adventuring trolls, and winged lizards, and creatures thriving under the depths of Sha.

Content and a bit hoarse, she leaned back in the chair. "I'm happy to see you."

"Of course, Blossom." He looked guilty. "I don't want you to go, but I guess you need to see this." Reaching into the side pocket on the chair where Dime was sitting, he handed her an envelope. "Don't read it here; it'll keep. Just promised I'd send it along."

She knew without asking that the letter was from Dayn, and a thread of tension, one she'd held without noticing, released in her mind. Dime had a feeling she should ask her father whether he was well, and if he'd come with her. But he'd always been capable on his own, as he was now. If he wasn't offering to go with her and hadn't gone with Dayn, there was a reason. She tucked the letter into her tunic.

An odd thought struck her. As whimsical as her father's creatures were, they never used valence.

"Da-da, what do you think of valence? Do you . . . think it's real?"

Her father was a strong believer in Sol's ways. She hoped the question wouldn't upset him.

For a second, she thought he wasn't listening. Then he turned toward her, a quirk to his smile. "My child." He paused. "The only thing I've ever known to be real is you. Valence? It must be how Sol brought you to me."

Dime could not respond. The stove clicked in the back room as they sat there, both staring at the lamp's light, flickering on the wall. Knowing she needed to go, she found it hard to rise from her chair.

"You ought to get going," he said. "You stop by anytime. Whatever you need, Blossom." She nodded.

With a final hug, still not finding any words, she picked up her bag and walked into the stairway, her father waving from the doorway until she'd made her way from his sight. Pausing in the stairway, for the first time since her original ordeal, she finally let herself cry. Then, dabbing her sleeve against her eyes, she took in a breath.

It was hard to find somewhere private to read a letter in the midst of the towers, not without spending the paynotes Ella had given her, ones she'd rather save until she needed them. There were parks, but any of the more secluded nooks wouldn't be in the lamplight, and her night vision wasn't enough to read by.

Finally, she settled on a curved street alley running between some shops, one that had several dozen delivery crates stacked into columns. The light from the windows shone down between them, but she hoped she was shielded from view. It looked like the sort of place a salespyr might step out to for a snack.

The letter did not have much to it; Dayn was wise enough to be vague.

> *Your friend says you are well. I am glad, and I look forward to hearing more of that story. He wouldn't go with us; you probably figured. We are fine. We're staying with someone recommended by A. If you recall our card group, that dome has a small residence in its top. If you go there, tell them who sent you. I miss you.*

Underneath, a little bouquet of flowers was drawn, with sort of a disproportional hand reaching out as if to offer them to her. Dime chuckled; he could *not* draw. She also smiled that he'd shaded in the hand. Guess she wasn't the only one self-conscious about age lately.

Beneath it waited a final note.

> *One sadness. The pyr who hums has been ill a while (I didn't know either) and his condition seems to be declining, enough that he has told friends. If you are able to visit him without gathering notice, it is unclear how long you'll have that opportunity.*

Dime let her hand fall forward, crinkling the note. He meant Zael, of course, who often hummed along, and not in tune, during musical performances. Dime and Dayn had joked about it the last time they'd all gone out. They weren't sure he even knew he was doing it, but there was no point in dampening his fun.

She'd known Zael a long time now; her first assignment back in the towers had been assisting him. Not directly assigned to the IC, he collected and compiled research conducted or proposed across the Circles as well as by private organizations. He studied these efforts, looking for links and recommending new projects to the Light's Circle.

They'd grown to be good friends over the cycles, not just Zael but his spouse Yorm. The four of them had often held biscuit together or taken in a show. He wasn't much older than Dime was, maybe five cycles. His knowing smile and narrow eyes flashed before her, happy and healthy in her mind.

Zael lived far uptown, not quite Nor Lodon, but close. Dime was eager to reach her family's side, but they were at least out of view for the time, hidden with Ador's help downcity. With Dayn's urging to do so, she could take the time to see Zael. And this put another stop right on the way, one she'd already gone back and forth about a dozen times in her mind. It was risky.

Yet, knowing Zael's troubles made her own feel less significant. It quelled her fear, her anxiety. Zael was a scholar, after all. He'd appreciate what she was considering. And she was going back that way anyway, now. It was a sign.

Dime struck a flint and held the paper out to catch fire, dropping it over a grate as the last corner fell into ash. Gathering her things, she took off in the direction of her old office.

Dime knew she couldn't just walk into the Circles' complex. Even if they'd let her in without incident, at best case she'd be prevented from reaching where she was trying to go. At worst case, she'd be ordered to stay, and then she'd really face a dilemma. And the complex was the last place one would ever attempt costuming themselves for the purpose of hiding.

She really was tired of hiding.

But, she reminded herself, until her children were safe, she'd have to push back her pride. So this was going to take some thought. The complex was busy, well-lit, and filled with pyrsi more observant than the meandering inhabitants of the residential towers. She turned from the curvy alley onto a wide street, doing her best to walk in the dark corners and not draw attention.

She couldn't think of a way in that wouldn't involve directly breaking code, and she wasn't sure she should take that kind of risk. But there had to be some way in. "Sol, send me a sign," she whispered, repeating her father's phrase.

Weaving around a brightly burning street lamp, she glanced at the advertisement illuminated beneath it, a trio of vertical banners hanging in a triangle shape from a metal stand, so the message could be viewed from all sides. *In the name of Ada-ji.*

So it came to be that Dime's short stature came into great bearing as she slid herself between the three banners, into the center space surrounded by metal poles and wide feet. She was at least relieved of her backpack's weight; the overloaded bag rested snug behind a bench.

Waiting for each break in pyrsi strolling or driving by, because certainly a floating advertisement would draw notice, she lifted the stand just off the ground and edged the whole thing—with herself hidden in the middle—a tower at a time away from the shopping area and up the hill toward the Circles' complex.

For a while, with no one in sight, she stepped out of the structure and carried it over her shoulder, balancing the poles as the banners flopped around. While she didn't like taking the sign, adorned with oversized sandwiches, away from where it'd been placed, advertisements like these were usually posted throughout the high city, and she'd only be garnering more visibility for it where she was going. So, hey, maybe it would help them.

When she finally got near the entry dome, she stepped back inside the banners. *Lettuce see how this goes.*

Extra officers stood around the entrances. While there were always a couple to verify that approaching pyrsi had Circles access, there had never been so many. She suspected they were watching for the same fairies that the Circles reassured pyrsi had not been seen. Dime shook her head, knowing the fairies could just fly up to any of the windows.

The bells sounded, and Dime stood in place, knowing there would be a surge of pyrsi arriving and leaving. A take or two later, the plaza had calmed back down.

Watching the officers to make sure they weren't looking her way, she sidled up to the corner of the walk. One of them turned toward her and stared, and she worried whether she'd been caught. She held as still as she could.

"Did you see that?" xe asked, pointing. "I didn't notice that before."

"Huh?" Xyr partner looked over, scrunching xyr eyebrows when xe saw the banners.

"Special on a new sandwich place. That's a good price."

"Oh, huh," the other said, turning back toward the street.

Having walked multiple times across Sol's lands, she was in much greater possession of patience than she could have claimed in her previous life. And so Dime waited, watching each group move by until a gap when no one was walking her way. Lifting up the poles, she waddled toward the building and stopped again.

The officers were still turned ahead, observing the pyrsi approaching the complex. Knowing that one had noticed the sign's previous location and not wanting xem to question xemself, she counted to five then ducked, banners and all, through the entrance way, setting her banners back down immediately alongside a display on the importance of reporting stone damage.

The entrance hall was always full of small exhibits, which the leadership placed throughout the path of the entering Circles work-force. With each pause in traffic, Dime moved again, positioning herself next to a different display in the large, busy hall. Near the back, she took a risk and popped into a side stairwell. Well, she couldn't go up the stairs like this.

With the stairwell wall to one side, she stepped out of the banners again, angling the signs forward against her other side, as if delivering them to the upper floors. She tilted the poles so the banners shielded her face from view as she climbed the stairs.

She managed this way over the course of several flights, feeling more like an agent than she ever had while working here. Sick of hiding but at least enjoying the irony, she beamed to herself a little from behind the banners.

There was a wide, windowed atrium ahead that opened into some of the back towers, home to more highly-regarded organiza-tions like the IC. During the day, the area was bathed in Sol's light, but now during nighttime, the lamps were lit, creating a dramatic corridor of light down the center and to the main stairs. It would be a difficult area to pass through unnoticed.

From the shadows of the corner stairwell, she peered out, seeing a familiar procession. *The Light! Sol!*

Sala herself was walking down from the back tower with its famous golden peak, where the Light's Circle met. Dime held her breath, thinking through the logistics. Sala would descend the big central staircase, not one here on the side. Her entourage would accompany her. And likely, anyone else in the area would pause, waiting for her to pass.

Despite the pounding of her heart, Dime told herself she was probably in less danger of being seen now than she had been before. Ironically, Sala would clear her path, at least into the IC tower.

With a few strides left before the procession drew near, Dime slid herself right next to the stairs, tucked away in the dark, angled corner.

She peered out as Sala walked through the atrium's center, still a distance away. Illuminated by the bright lamplight, the Light looked as Dime remembered her, though it had been a while since she'd seen the powerful fe'pyr closer than from the audience of an amplified speech in the plaza. Through their many tattoos, Sala's temples and cheeks boasted all levels of honor, accolade, and rank.

Her suit, a variegated gray with smooth yellow accents, was made by her own clothing brand. Selling branded clothes had always seemed to Dime a perfectly normal thing for a high-class pyr to do. Now, better understanding the secrets of the world and with a sense of real potential peril, the symbolism took on a rawness that Dime had not considered.

Ferala, for all his fresh tea and cowardice, had at least acknowledged that peril. Yet given all the Light's influence, it felt like she put more energy into designing clothes than she did understanding Ada-ji's problems. And no better if she was merely suggesting and approving designs, then giving them her name.

Dime did appreciate the way the soft colors glowed in the lamplight as well as the subtle movement of the tailored segments, enough to catch a hint of movement but not swaying with bold beauty as Volana's ribbons had under the trees of Pito.

Wearing her self-branded suit, the Light strode across the large space, looking forward but having a casual conversation with one of the clerks to her side. Sala's huge platform shoes held her visibly above the others. Dime watched the way the clerks walked, close enough to respond yet always keeping a small distance behind. The procession reminded Dime of Tikinal's giant mop—Sala was the steady handle and everyone else twirled and moved with her.

Dime considered that fate had just handed her the opportunity to stop the Light as she had the High Seat. With time passing quickly, she knew she had to pick one outcome: confront Sala or make it into the records section. She would not be able to do both.

She could meet with Sala in the future if she needed to. She probably wouldn't get another throw at records once Sala knew she was around. Or even, alive. No, she was staying with her plan.

From between two of the oiled canvas banners, Dime peered at the leader of all Ja-lal. And let her pass. With a shaky breath, she made sure the last footsteps had faded and then slid along the wall from behind her signs, thankful for the gap in traffic Sala's entourage had created.

Seeing the entrance to the IC tower gave Dime a little jolt. Entirely because it didn't. How many times had she walked through this door? It was common, familiar. Like she'd never left. That upset her in ways she didn't have time to understand.

Gathering resolve, she slipped back inside the triangular signs, moving in stages down the elevated walkway and then through the maze of halls and offices. Finally getting close to the IC records section, she stopped abruptly at a noise, clattering the base of the stand down as a couple approached the small lobby. Fervently, she hoped they hadn't heard her.

"Huh," said a fe'pyr Dime recognized. Seeing a familiar face, even if not one close to her, gave her a flutter of instability, like the time-traveling merchant in a story she'd read a while back. Coming back here, after leaving, she felt like that merchant. Everything the same, yet everything different. Dime, out of place.

Except she had no time portal, no way to whisk away at signs of trouble. Like the one in front of her. The fe'pyr pointed right at Dime's signs.

"Spicy Sandwiches. What's that?"

"What do you mean, what's that? It's a sandwich that's spicy."

"I know, but you don't call a sandwich by its flavor; you call it by its ingredients. You know, you can have a spicy stew, but not a spicy sandwich."

"I have no idea what you're talking about," her companion, someone Dime didn't recognize, said. "Oh, but that's a good deal. We should try it sometime."

The fe'pyr leaned in, peering at the finely lettered text. "It's a little downcity. Guess they're trying to bring in the Circles crowd. Sure, we'll try it sometime. That *is* a good deal. Get us out of here for a while. Oh, look, hullnut dein and hot peppers. Yes, please."

Discussing when would be a good time to skip out for sandwiches, the couple walked through the doorway and out onto a sky alley connecting the adjacent tower.

Abandoning the banners, Dime sped through the halls, done with being a sandwich ad and knowing the apparatus would stick out too much anyway in the narrow hallways beyond.

She was far into the complex here, a notion that weighed more heavily on her as she walked briskly toward her destination.

"Dime?"

She froze, reassuring herself that she recognized the voice. And it was a friendly one. Dime spun on her heels to face Jenn.

"Are you ok?" ve asked.

"Yeah, hey." Dime glanced around nervously, and Jenn smiled.

"I'm sorry if I scared you, but I wanted to say hi. Here, let's get out of the hall." Jenn opened a meeting room and swung closed the curtains after they walked in. Dime always thought these rooms were funny; they installed interior windows so pyrsi could see who was in the room, then whoever was in the room always covered the windows.

"Are you ok?" Jenn asked.

"Yeah, just skittish. Pretty sure I'm not allowed to be here."

"Are you doing anything I should be concerned about?"

"Here? No."

Jenn's expression shifted to one less cheerful and more concerned. "We've missed you."

"Oh, it hasn't been so long." Dime smiled, but it wasn't possible Jenn hadn't heard the rumors. Maybe she was too nervous to talk about it. "So . . ." Dime made a clicking sound with her tongue.

"I have to admit," Jenn said, "I knew you were adventurous, but escaping fairies was not on the list of things I'd considered."

Dime laughed. "You know what, me either! I promise! Hey," she offered. "Something important. And there's a lot of backstory, so I hope you'll trust me. Anyway, I don't really know how to summarize it, but . . . the fairies aren't like how we say."

"Oh, no, the Circles never spin things to their advantage. We're much too honest!" Ve stood and put vis hands on vis waist like a fictional hero before relaxing again.

Dime noticed discomfort in vis eyes.

"But, I mean, the Great War did happen, right? And you aren't like . . . associated with them?" Jenn chuckled nervously.

"No, no. I mean, yes, I mean—" Dime tried to gather herself. "I didn't even know if they were real. They are. That's definitive. As far as the Great War, it's getting fuzzier; I mean, what do we even know about it? We're afraid of something we don't talk about. Look, the important thing is, don't believe what you hear. They're not all good either. Fairies, I mean. Some are dangerous. And their pyrsi—they truly are pyrsi—are being told the same level of awful things about us that we're told about them. Seems wrong, right? Stay away from them or we'll have to fight, but, like, isn't that literally encouraging fighting?"

"*Hmm.*" Jenn didn't seem to know what to say to that. Dime probably hadn't made any sense and it was a lot to spring on someone in the middle of a random work shift. Ve hefted up the notebooks ve was holding, readjusting them. "Hey, ok, you're probably sneaking in somewhere. Sorry, I didn't mean to bust your confidence about it. It's just, we really do miss you around here. It was nice to see you; I got excited."

"I miss you all too." Dime was surprised that she meant it. She'd spent so long blocking thoughts of work, and the Circles, it felt a little invasive to let them creep back in. But, she supposed, there were many more good memories than bad. "Except Atti. I don't miss Atti."

If Jenn was going to say anything in his defense, a look at Dime's face stopped ver. "He's challenging. Anyway, guess you have to go? Can I help? If you want, I'll tell you when the way is clear. Give you a little more chance?" Ve winked.

"Sure." She almost added that ve was a great accomplice, but she didn't know how far the joking could go before she crossed a line. Jenn trusted her, though, and that boosted her confidence. "Thanks," she added.

Jenn seemed to have more to say, but maybe ve realized the risk of being caught here with her. Her rambling didn't seem to help either. "Hey. Good luck, Dime. I'll remember what you said. If it comes up. I promise. I'll . . . think about it."

"Thanks. May I hug you?" Dime couldn't believe she'd asked it, but it would be more awkward to take it back. *Hugging coworkers!*

"Of course!" Jenn leaned forward with a polite hug, patting Dime's back and then standing back. Just as the invisible thread of tension regarding Dayn's safety had snapped, another snapped. Permission to remember her former career. To embrace it. Even if the embrace was rather business-like. Dime remembered, here, how many good pyrsi she'd worked with. How many good memories. Friends like Jenn, who lifted pyrsi up. Atti and the others who held pyrsi down, maybe they weren't worth remembering.

Jenn moved toward the door. "It was so nice to see you. I'll be watching for you. Not here. In general."

Dime didn't have the focus to consider all the conflicting emotions circling through her. But she trusted Jenn back. Trusted ve wouldn't tell anyone she was here. At least not yet. "Hey, thanks. So much."

"No, no problem." Jenn seemed to think the thanks was for the looking out, as ve slipped into the hall and tried to appear casual, flipping through a notebook like ve was searching for the right page. Dime could hear several pyrsi walking by, some offering greetings as they passed. Without warning, Jenn tapped on the glass. Dime stepped through the door. "Go," ve whispered. Dime didn't wait.

The path was only clear for a couple of hallways, and then Dime zipped past a few pyrsi, none of whom seemed to notice who they were passing. Her breath faster now, she broke into a near-run, before turning into the records office. Darting down the first hall, she rushed into the clerks' hub. Of the four desks in the room, only one was occupied.

"Beb!" Dime said, hoping some goodwill from her past remained. Beb was the hardest-working clerk she'd ever met, and Dime had often put in a good word about her. Though, maybe Beb didn't know that.

Beb steadied herself, leaning forward with her hands against the desk. "Agent Dime?"

"I know. I'm not supposed to be here. And I'm not an agent anymore. But I hope that you'll trust me; I need your help." The records clerk stood slowly, her legs appearing to wobble a tiny bit, based on the shaking of her soft peach suit. Dime couldn't just jump in and scare the pyr like this. "A lot has happened, I know."

"You could say that." Beb peered at Dime, as if not sure who she was seeing.

"I don't want to pry, but, uh, the Light's Circle can't be happy about what happened." Dime was used to bantering with Dayn and Ador about Sala and the others by name, but knew she couldn't be so direct here.

"No, not happy. I don't know what's real or rumor—and I'd prefer not to talk about it—but the fuel it's given to Sol's Pillars is no boon."

Dime wanted to respect Beb's request not to discuss events, but she needed to offer her some reassurance so she wouldn't shoo Dime out. "I won't tell you. But I didn't cause it, and now I'm trying to help." Beb didn't look terribly reassured.

Dime kept talking, hoping she could learn a little first. "About Sol's Pillars—what have they been doing in the city? I saw the crowds at the gates; are they just, riling pyrsi?"

"They say they're standing watch for the fairies. But, from everything I've heard, they're harassing pyrsi just trying to pass in and out of the city. Pressuring them to join or donate. Telling them—" Beb's nose wrinkled in distaste.

"The same old things?" Dime had no issue condemning what she considered the harmful speech they spread around. All she ever thought they cared about was maintaining their rank and perks in the city. Holding down pyrsi who'd made mistakes. She'd always thought they were gross. The fairy thing was just a front for their views, anyway. It irritated her immensely that they could now pretend it had always been the issue, like they'd known.

"Yes. But not the same old pyrsi. Not just the usual high-class group, it's common pyrsi as well now. Pyrsi I never thought would buy into it. And the volume has increased." Beb was being polite; the enthusiasm with which the Sol's Pillars had responded to Dime's own act outside the walls disgusted her.

"What about Jaza?" The IC had kept a watch on the pyr for ages; she was known to be the primary force behind the group. And a powerful speaker, too. She'd be hard to miss—known for bright makeup and colorful clothing, her loud rallies always skirted what the Circles would tolerate. Dime didn't know what they'd do about her now.

Jaza seemed angry enough; now emboldened by the fairies' arrival, she might just take a hemsa and keep rallying. And what, then? Mark her followers one by one? Actually— The core members of Sol's Pillars wore tattoos proclaiming their affiliation—maybe the hemsa would have no effect, turning instead into a badge of honor.

Her own mind had recently expanded to consider these sorts of options, but she most definitely was not going to mention them to Beb.

"She's been quiet," Beb mused. "The agents believe Jaza's still behind it all, but she hasn't been out herself yet. I suppose that's a good sign. Maybe this will all go away." She glanced at Dime, looking quickly down again.

Dime needed to be careful. "I don't want to cause any trouble," she said. "I'd like your help finding some records." Beb looked uncertain, and Dime smiled, trying to project a sense of normalcy. "Then I'll be leaving."

Beb seemed to regain her composure. "Honestly, Dime, whatever you've been wrapped up in, I don't need to be a part." Dime made no motion to leave, and Beb hesitated. "I don't know what's here that could be too interesting, though, so if you'll not mention it, I can help direct you."

"I'm looking for birth records from the cycle I was born. Just . . . something I need to see."

"The whole cycle?" Beb said. "That's a lot of records."

"We still have them? I mean, you do?" *Of course they do.* "I'll try not to take long. So I can go."

With a long sigh, Beb escorted Dime back through a maze of tiny passages and half-floors to a room full of cabinets. "They start here," she said. "I need to go back up front."

For a moment, Dime considered asking for a promise that Beb wouldn't tell anyone. But Dime didn't want to start mistrusting pyrsi she'd known for cycles, nor give the clerk a reason to mistrust her. Dime had spent a long time here, doing what the leadership wanted from her. She'd—

Realizing Beb had already left, Dime took a breath and started paging through the files. First, she'd want to look at her own. See if it held clues. The records were in birth order, and she paged through to the date she'd always celebrated as her birthturn, thinking now it was when he found her.

Diamond. The date was listed, but no time. A section titled *Natal Record* was left blank. Oh, right. She remembered seeing that on Luja's birth record when they'd updated vis parental info. It was a test conducted by a medic at the time of birth to ensure the ba'pyr had no time-sensitive treatment needs.

She'd been there when they conducted Tum's; the medic had thanked the pyr giving birth for getting there in time to record one. So, a ba'pyr left by Neimano would have no record; xyr file would have been placed later by whoever had taken the position as parent and had registered xyr child.

Her finger ran down the paper, stopping on the parental info. *Ma'Gorg.* His residence, same as it was now. *Profession: Maintenance Circle.* A line was scrawled across the notes section: *Unclaimed. (Poss. haven.) No health issues.* There was nothing else of interest . . . but what was she expecting? A large note that said, *Wing Scars*?

Returning to the front, she flipped through the files one by one, looking only for any missing natal exams or any unusual marks in the notes section, which was almost always left blank. She skipped records with a death date on top. It was better to let the dead rest in peace, she believed. Or maybe she just didn't want to know.

The few she found without a natal record confirmed her theory; there was usually a note explaining that the ba'pyr was born at home, or that the parent had opted out of an exam. In all cases, the event of a birth was referenced.

None of the records had *Fairy* in large letters or anything else that would have made the job easier. But she also remembered the ba'pyrsi had been left in places of influence. If the clues pointed away from another of the . . . well, Ferala had called them *diamonds* but she didn't like that— If the clues pointed away from a Project Diamondsong *victim,* she moved past that file. If any looked like a fit, she wrote down the details on a note and stuck it back in her pocket.

Her fingers raw from the scratchy paper, she finally reached records a full cycle away from her own. She closed the drawer and looked at her sheet. Only three names. *Kolk. Cren. Nafat.*

Three out of five. Maybe she'd missed the others. But she couldn't go through the files again. She thought she'd ruled the rest out, or at least they'd shown no clues. She'd done the best she could.

Winding her way back to where Beb sat, still alone, thankfully, Dime held the paper tight. "If I have the registration numbers of three pyrsi, could I get their current addresses?"

"Dime," Beb groaned.

"I know. I promise I'm not trying to get you in trouble. I'll . . . I'll tell them you had nothing to do with it if anyone finds out." Beb's eyes widened. Dime's view had shifted so much recently, she forgot how much that might sound like an attempt to deceive. She didn't think she meant it that way.

"I mean, I'll clarify that I'm responsible for this. Please, Beb. Isn't it better if I don't tell you the details?" Dime almost promised she'd do no harm, but remembered how harsh that would sound to Beb's ears. And she couldn't promise what she was doing was something the Circles would appreciate; that probably wasn't true. "I hope you can trust me. I'm sorry I can't say more."

Secrets. Well, the Circles were used to those.

Eyes narrowed, Beb walked toward the back and asked Dime, without turning around, for the three registration numbers. Dime wasn't comfortable revealing them, but she didn't want to give Beb any reason for distrust. She read them off.

After a short search, Beb handed her a folded sheet, her hands shaking. "One earned a hemsa and left Lodon. No street code, just confirmed to be up in the mountains. Here are the other two."

"Did it say what the hemsa was for?"

Beb shivered. "Yes, some sort of . . . explosion. Pyrsi were *hurt.*" Dime knew how difficult that answer had been to give; the Violence never happened, so there shouldn't be a record of it. She really needed to go.

"Keeping so much information on pyrsi. It bothers me." Dime stopped, not having meant to say it aloud. She wasn't against records; she really just meant they raised such potential for abuse.

Beb stepped back. "You were a good manager and pyrsi spoke

well of you. But you were a part of this for a long time, and now you come back, amidst all *the rumors*, ask for records, and then lecture me about keeping them? You know what, I'm just doing my job, and not all of us have the luxury of leaving ours. You got your records; now you need to leave."

Luxury? Choice wasn't a luxury. Forcing a pyr into one specific role, that was how the Fo-ror saw it. Not Dime.

Still, she'd pushed Beb too far. Beb would probably keep quiet about Dime being here, but she couldn't rely on her not calling someone back if she stayed any longer.

"Beb, I'm sorry. I wish I could say more." Dime hesitated. "You don't want me to. Ok?"

Beb nodded. "Are you done?"

"I'm leaving. I promise. I could really use a map to help me do that. Do you have one of the older ones? It doesn't need to be current, I just . . . need to get out of here for a while. Like you said, you want things to settle. Do you have one of the older versions?" Dime knew they kept the older maps around a little while, to give to agents on assignment who might not bring them back in good shape.

With tight lips, Beb turned to the wood bench behind her desk, where Dime could see stacks of items, probably staged for filing or disposal. Walking around to meet her, Dime scanned the bench, noting a bag of pencils, stacks of old maps, and a few crates with what looked like newly inked maps. The word *Boring* caught her eye.

Beb turned back toward Dime and whipped one of the old maps forward in her hands. Dime took it and spread it partially on the desk. Folding it back toward the Great Cliff, she searched to make sure this was an agent map, one with the dens. She tapped the small symbol then folded it back up. With a grateful nod to Beb, she slipped the map in the same side pocket with the letter, names, and addresses.

She almost didn't mention the crates.

"Are those the Boring locations?" Now Beb looked furious. "It's ok; my spouse works for the Construction Circle."

"Then I'm sure your spouse knows what's Circles business." Beb softened her expression. "Dime, you don't work here. I know that's awkward, but you're the one who did it. And I don't believe what they say, but—put yourself in my shoes. What if I'm not supposed to be helping you? I respect you, but I'm not losing my job or my status over this. Please leave."

Dime considered her words, realizing that Beb would have called Enforcement right when she'd walked in if there had been orders to do so. And she seemed in full denial about the Fo-ror, or at least she didn't want to know. Dime felt sure the Circles were watching for her, but if so, it was a specific order, not a broad one. Were the extra officers outside looking for the fairies, or for her? Or for Sol's Pillars? Maybe all of it.

"Beb, thank you. I wish you well."

"I wish you well also. Agent Dime?"

Dime didn't like the look on Beb's face.

"I'm feeling unsure about the last few takes, and I'd like to forget them. Please. Don't come back."

"I won't bother you again." Dime gave a polite nod.

Dime did not rush on her way out, as she had a sudden need for Beb to see her leave with calm, deliberate steps, her head held high.

Two victims. Dime had two names and two locations. Previously abstract, these were real pyrsi now. With Dime refusing to cooperate, either one could be at risk of a visit from Neimano, if he hadn't approached them already. Without knowing, she had to find them. Warn them. And her conscience wouldn't let her wait to do it.

Also, her friend was ill. She would see him too. Talking to Jenn had cemented that; Dime loved these pyrsi who had shared the cycles with her, and she would see Zael before she left.

Dayn, keep everyone safely out of view. I will be there soon.

Keeping her senses alert, Dime turned each corner, waited, and moved along. As she stepped into the quiet lobby where her sandwich sign still proclaimed the joy of spicy sandwiches and where to get one, she was stunned to see a group of pyrsi standing there, gathered around it.

"Dime," one gasped. "Dime! What are you doing here?" The face, somewhat familiar, smiled, looking excited to see her. Next to xem, one of the others screamed. Bolting right through the center of the group, Dime dodged to avoid the sign and spun back around, sliding indelicately into the stairwell.

She ran.

Interlude

"Eat your meal," ve growled, as two of vis children tussled on the floor, and the third continued to tattle. "All of you, *sit down.*"

Aivi was on edge, admittedly. The Wes Gate promenade had been an exciting place to live. Small towers dotted its streets like the fancier neighborhoods upcity, yet rooms were available to lower-class pyrsi like verself, due to the unpredictable traffic of the Wes Gate that kept anyone away who was particular about needing a few bells of quiet.

Now, ve was starting to think they were right.

Ever since that silly rumor about fairies in Lodon, the Sol's Pillars had been gathering here, up and down the street leading to the gate, and all measures of outside. Aivi had no idea what they were hoping to find. Ve didn't believe in fairies, and even if ve did, wouldn't they just fly in? Not bother with the dustbin of conspiracists banging pans together like ba'pyrsi?

Vis youngest began to cry. "Sit down to *eat,*" ve ordered.

Aivi's spouse was late again. Ve wouldn't blame her; she said it was getting harder and harder to make her deliveries in the area, working through crowded streets and getting stopped for recruitment every two steps. "I'm here every turn the same," she told Aivi she'd protested. "I think I've got the message."

As ve turned around with a sizzling pan of sliced purpleplant, a ball rolled across the floor and nearly tripped ver, and Aivi spun and tilted to keep the hot dish from spilling across the room. Setting it back on the stove, ve howled at the burn on vis hand. Aivi closed vis eyes and concentrated, like vis mother had always taught ver, and willed the burn to heal. It felt like it helped, so ve stuck to the tradition, whether it did or not.

The oldest had taken the hint at the near-disaster, and sat at the table, suddenly a model of behavior. The other two, oblivious, continued to toss the ball back and forth. One climbed on a chair, a napkin tucked into the back of his shirt and, waving his arms in the air.

"What. Are. You. Doing." Aivi grunted.

He looked up with a grin. "We're playing fairies!"

The door opened, and vis spouse walked in, a tired look on her face. She took one scan around the room. "I've got it," she said with a weak smile. "Just sit down."

From outside, the Sol's Pillars took up a new chant. And Aivi thought, not caring that it was wildly inappropriate, that if the fairies didn't return to scare them off, ve would.

Act 2

THE TOWERS

Dime's second departure from the Circles' complex was a bit more dramatic than her first. Knowing her presence was no longer a secret yet unable to imagine that anyone here would try to physically stop her, Dime darted through the rooms and corridors and kept her focus trained on reaching the main doors.

She'd known it would only be a matter of time until she was recognized and word got out, but she'd needed to make it to records first, and she'd done that. Right now, there were two priorities: getting out of here before she had to overtly disobey a Circles' order, which could cause all kinds of complications, and then managing to hide again in the city, to buy the rest of the time she needed before getting out altogether.

Bouncing between the displays of the long entrance hall and then out through one of the many wide doors, she heard the officers shouting to her as she barreled past. She didn't stop to listen.

As she reached the bench where she'd stowed her backpack, she tugged at the overloaded bag, wrenching it free and heaving it onto her back.

Her muscles began to ache as she ran down the street, turned a corner, and ducked between a section of towers, finally stopping in a garden to catch her breath. The winding path through the small office garden was lit with tall lamps, but the dark section of trees in the back shielded her from view. She collapsed onto the soft ground, breathing heavily as she stared up into the branches.

Even these few cultivated trees seemed empty now, short and pruned, without the sounds of pyrsi flying between them. She felt more secure, here in Lodon, knowing anyone looking for her would not be able to fly. That had not been the case, of course, when she'd first fled.

After she'd left Lodon the first time, it felt like no matter how many ways she found to turn or take cover or even travel across the entirety of the plains, every time she was back in the open, there they'd be again: flying fairies waving their ropes. With a clearer mind, now, she suspected they'd used some sort of valence to track or find her. It just wasn't possible they were that lucky. She would have realized it at the time, but her thoughts had been so muddled in the escape.

Having been prohibited from any true discussions of valence throughout her life—only warnings that the wicked fairies bore foul insect wings that created it—she had no idea how valence was generated, used, or controlled. The criticality of that information to the Ja-lal stunned her, in the sense they had not pursued it.

So. The secret was out. Dime was in town. She sighed, finally sitting back up.

While the urgency of getting to her family stayed first on her mind, she wasn't sure when she'd have a chance to be back in the city. Dayn's note had suggested they were in hiding, presumably staying with pyrsi Ador trusted. She needed to get to them soon and get them out, but she knew it would take the Circles some time to organize a search. She could make a few more stops, if she hurried.

She'd planned to see Zael next, but realized she'd subconsciously run back in the direction of her own former home, very close to Ador. So, she'd see them both, though quickly. And what about the two pyrsi whose names she carried, the potential other victims of Neimano's plot?

Dime pulled the small papers from her pocket, with information she'd jotted from the birth records as well as Beb's notes from the address file. She was nervous about visiting these strangers and disrupting their lives. If it were strictly a matter of whether they had the right to know their history and biology versus the right to live their lives without the burden of this knowledge, she'd likely debate it all night.

But they could be in danger. Neimano had come for her; he might come for the other victims as well, if he hadn't already. She would have to warn them; she saw no other choice. Both addresses were farther downcity, as were Dayn and her children. Logistically, it made sense to make the two upcity stops first: Ador and Zael.

Dime's increasing number of "quick stops" reminded her of shopping at the market. She always went in for one thing, and always thought, *well, while I'm here—* And that reminded her: she really was hungry. Chewing a spicy fruit stick and trying to push aside her memories of poor, intoxicated Deberele—well, hopefully he'd at least enjoyed his snack—Dime stood and stretched.

A mural across the garden drew her eye, its colorful depictions of hackberry boughs brightening the tower's old stones in the lamplight. She doubted any of the pyrsi here had any idea the sprawling plants were real, thriving in the Heartland. Even her own city was different now, seen with new eyes. Pensive, she walked away.

While she did avoid large crowds or bright lights as she crossed the two streets over, Dime didn't take the time to hide. As long as anyone spotting her was unprepared and not overly motivated, she felt she could slip away. It was a more coordinated effort she feared, and that wouldn't be pulled together in the next bell or two. Moving quickly was more important now. Thankfully, pyrsi were going about their business and not looking her way.

As she walked past her own tower and closer to seeing her friend, for Ador lived in the same neighborhood, her anticipation grew. Working for the Circles, she'd needed to keep a distance from his organization, the Free Winds. The Circles categorized them as a potentially destabilizing force, working counter to pyrsi's interests. Dime had surmised that the Free Winds challenged the way the Circles ran Lodon and Sol's Reach, drafting and garnering support for new ideas, then presenting those to the Circles. As long as it stayed at only a little meeting and grumbling, the Circles kept an eye on them but otherwise let them be.

Understanding that what she knew of them from the IC was likely biased, and what she knew of them from rumor was likely incomplete, she looked forward to talking to Ador directly and learning more. He couldn't help her with the Fo-ror, but Ador might know things on the Ja-lal side that could help her decide what to do next. They wouldn't have enough time to talk in-depth now, but she could at least get some ideas and then tell him where to find her, once she left the city.

Pyrsi were busy in the tower; a few started at recognizing her, but Dime continued on, and no one tried to stop her. She did wait for a lull in traffic to walk the final couple of flights upward, to avoid being seen entering Ador's home. She knocked on the door.

It opened slowly, and Dime worried that something was wrong. Peeking around the side, Batu broke into a huge smile. "Come in, come in, hurry." Batu ushered Dime in, shutting the door behind them. "Dime! Ador said you were well, but to see you myself brings such joy!"

As sleek and tailored as Ador's fashion sense was, his spouse's had always been a friendly joke between Dayn and her, a frequent discussion point after having stopped by for a game or a biscuit. It wasn't that it was important or that they meant any disrespect, but the contrast between Ador and his spouse amused them in an endearing way.

Batu's big colors and bright floral patterns were cheerful and bold, but always a little off to the eye. Dime loved it; she loved the freedom with which Batu dressed, whether it always worked or not. Today, she wore a wide floral sash, wrapped around her suit and tied in a tight knot at the side, as if the fabric wasn't quite long enough but she'd just managed to fasten it.

Loose sashes were uncommon in the city, especially one so wide. Just the suggestion that a swath could be wrapped around someone's head or face was too close to the idea of a hood for most; no one wanted to be accused of rebellion.

Unless, perhaps, you were married to the leader of the largest critical voice in the land. Or, as she now understood it, in Sol's Reach.

Batu continued to beam as she helped Dime take off her backpack and showed her to a chair. "Ador isn't here, but I wish he were. He'd be so happy to see you. I don't think he'll be back for a few bells, though; he was meeting someone downcity."

Dime's heart fell, and she tried not to let it show on her face. Those last few steps up here, she'd felt such a longing to see her friend. A friend who she'd always appreciated, but who she now understood she hadn't appreciated enough. Of course, it wasn't even about asking him questions, she really just wanted to see him.

"I can't stay, though I'll take a drink of water. And if you could refill my flask . . ." Dime pulled the flask out of the bag's side pocket. Batu had whisked it from her hand almost before she'd fully lifted it. Dime sat back in the seat.

"Of course, of course, anything you need. I'm so glad you're well. We've all been so worried." Only then did Batu's expression waver. Dime understood; it wouldn't be easy to casually ask about a friend's involvement in something that must have changed the very nature of Ador's work, probably making it much more difficult.

"It really was fairies." Dime cringed at the implicit omission, even before she made it. Though biology was never something one needed to reveal without cause, she considered whether she was being dishonest with her close friends by not sharing what she'd learned about herself, and how it was impacting her now. She probably would tell them, she realized, but not before telling Dayn. He deserved to know first.

"They're real," she continued. "I'm not so happy with the ones who burst into my home"—Batu nodded in understanding—"but the rest of them are mostly like us."

"Oh, yes," Batu agreed. Dime was surprised at how casually she accepted this.

"You and Ador, you believe in fairies?"

It was Batu who now hesitated. Dime's questions must sound bold for someone who had just left the Circles and had generally avoided political discussions with friends. Yet, Batu would never imagine the last few turns she'd lived. Dime could, then, give her some idea.

"I've been to their lands," Dime offered. She didn't know how else to convey that she was safe to talk to—that her world had changed.

The way she said it seemed to surprise Batu as much as it put her at ease. "Have you, now? Oh, wonderful! Then, yes, you must talk to Ador. We do believe in fairies; we believe in someturn reaching out to them. Many cycles, the Free Winds have discussed this." There was clearly more, but Dime wouldn't push.

Batu took the flask and disappeared through a door.

The IC knew the Free Winds disagreed with aspects of Circles' policy and led discussions on ways it could be changed. Dime hadn't known that the Free Winds had discussed the fairies, not exactly in the open, but openly at all. She pushed back familiar feelings of frustration at how much she hadn't known and how simple, it turned out, it would have been to have learned more.

Batu returned, handing Dime a cup of water and her refilled flask. "What is it like? If I may ask?"

Dime didn't have to ask what she meant. In fact, seeing Batu's eyes cloud with awe made Dime feel uncomfortable, though she couldn't pinpoint why. She shouldn't worry; she trusted Batu as she did Ador and, by the gleam in Batu's expression, this was probably something she'd considered for a very long time.

"Like the towers of Lodon, the trees of Pito have life at every layer. Dirt paths wind around the wide trunks, with gardens and storage and room for little creatures to run and hop. Above that, wooden walkways swirl around treeborne structures and turn to meet each other, like the crossing alleys and walkways of our towers.

Above that, the birds sing and the leaves rattle and somewhere up there, the daylight of Sol or the nightlight of the skystones peeks through, dancing its way to the ground."

She stopped, noting Batu's distant gaze.

"It sounds mesmerizing," Batu said, her voice taking a sing-song tone. "When . . . when we get back together, I'd love to hear more."

Dime smiled. "Maybe someturn you'll visit. You and Ador." Hearing the words from her own mouth, Dime wasn't sure they were responsible. Would there be such a world? Should there be? Dime had to remind herself that, as much as her perspective had recently changed, life had stayed mostly the same for the majority of pyrsi.

She couldn't just pop back into town and spout out things that would have floored her just eight turns ago.

Batu rested her hands on her hips, not appearing shocked or troubled by the comment. "I'd like that," she said. With a quick change of expression, she clapped her hands together. "But you said you had to go. Is there anything else you need?"

Dime finished the cup of water and handed it back. "I'd only like to get word to Ador; I think we have much to discuss."

Batu nodded as though Dime had said something quite serious. "Yes, you do. Did you . . . hear where your family is?"

"I did," Dime said. "I'll go there soon. Batu, there's an IC den where I plan to take them for a while. The agents despise going there, and it's desolate anyway, so I hope it'll give me time to plan. If Ador doesn't mind the trip, he could meet us there." Dime unfolded the map from its pocket and pointed to the location. "Could you tell him?" Telling Batu felt safer than leaving a note that could be found.

"I will; I will." Batu stared at the map, running her finger down it like she was being given a very important mission. Well, she was.

"And how are you, Batu? How are lessons?" Dime wanted to be polite; Batu loved talking about her career.

"They've been a bit disrupted lately, I'll admit. The students, of course. They have no proper fear of the Circles at that age; they've been going on and on about fairies ever since—"

"No, it's ok. No one knows what to call it." She still wasn't over Ella calling it her Big Adventure, but she wasn't going to mention that. "Let's say since my departure." It seemed a polite term, but Dime wasn't interested in upsetting Batu by calling it what she considered it: an attack.

"Yes, since your departure. I'm telling you, the syrup doesn't go back in the squeezebag, especially with our imaginative youth. The Circles will have their work cut out for them, squashing this."

"What do you think?" Dime couldn't help but ask. "Will it be squashed?"

Batu frowned. "I would say that depends on what happens next. If the answer is nothing, there is a slight chance." She hesitated. "But with Agent Dime running around town telling pyrsi that fairies are real and she's been to their treehouse city?" She leaned in and whispered, "Probably not."

Dime let out a long breath. "You may be right. There's a lot I don't know. Just, whatever happens, know you can trust me."

Batu tilted her head. "We would always trust you, Dime. Never doubt that."

Warmth crept into Dime's heart. "I won't."

Feeling dazed and suddenly realizing a wrapped stack of crackers was resting in her hand, Dime said a polite goodbye to Batu and headed back down the stairs. "Hello," she waved to a couple of residents who were unabashedly staring her way. "Nice night!"

Dime varied her path on the way out, not staying in any one view for too long. Zael's tower wasn't too far from here, yet it would be two or three takes of a walk. Her backpack weighed on her shoulders, and she stretched them back.

As she crunched down the herb-laced crackers, she gave serious consideration to renting a toothcar, but didn't want to risk it so close to the complex. If anyone from the Circles was looking for her, they'd be checking the cars. She'd wait until she wasn't so upcity, but Sol, she'd had enough walking.

Zael's tower was uncrowded. It was an older style of tower,

with fewer common areas, and so pyrsi were mostly inside, with any mingling occurring in the ground garden. Dime greeted the few pyrsi she passed on the stairs, but they were absorbed or distracted, not noticing or understanding who she was.

Dime's hand wavered as she reached to knock on the door. Zael was a Gamh, like Dime, though a few cycles older. Not old enough to be so ill. She wasn't used to seeing pyrsi in her own epoch with an extended illness, or at least not already on the mend. And Zael was a good friend.

Zael's spouse answered the door, standing stunned as she saw the visitor.

"Yorm, hi. Sorry to surprise you this way. I heard about Zael and I wanted to say hello to him. Let him know I'm ok and he's on my mind. If you're concerned about . . . everything else, please don't worry, I just want to see him. I'm not here for any trouble."

Yorm continued to stand in silence before finally replying. "I'm sorry; I'm being so rude."

"No, no," Dime answered, "I understand. There's a whole story, as you can imagine. It's not why I'm here. And I won't burden you with it."

"Dime?" a voice wheezed from inside. "Dime? Yorm, let her in. Please."

Yorm's smile wasn't entirely welcoming, but she escorted Dime into their sleeping room, where Zael rested back against the headboard of their bed, surrounded by pillows. His face was gaunt, but otherwise he looked as he normally did. He set down a book.

On the side of Zael's forehead, in front of his many other tattoos, was a tiny hemsa. He was the only pyr Dime had ever known to work in the Circles with a hemsa at all, however small, and it was especially odd given his long-standing reputation for high integrity and insightful work.

The symbol marked him for trespassing and danger to property, with an extra mark for insubordination to Enforcement. Danger to property probably meant he'd actually damaged something—it was hard to know in Circles' speak. He'd told her once it was back in his Aoch; he'd not really been grown. Pyrsi always winced when they first saw it, but those who knew him had become used to it.

Dime never had. Not in judgment of Zael, but for whoever had decided he deserved it.

Yorm left, closing the door behind her.

"Don't get mad at her. She's been through a lot lately. And, you know, they say you're one of the fairies now."

Dime's laugh to that came off a little nervous. "Oh, I consider myself an independent faction." She tried to smile.

Zael's chuckle turned into a cough. "Dime, you were always an independent faction. If you've come around to realize it, I'm tickled. Oh, and thank you."

Dime returned a quizzical look.

"It's just, you've been in here, what, a good ten strides, and you haven't told me I'm going to be fine. Just wanted to thank you for that."

Dime groaned. Even in her perfectly normal health, Tum sometimes had to endure the same sort of overly-positive comments from pyrsi. She hadn't thought how it might be amplified around someone who was ill. Let alone being potentially terminal, which Dayn's note had clearly suggested.

"What's worse is they tell me how strong I am, as if it's on me to beat it. It gets old." He glanced at Dime, as if trying to decide whether to say something.

She knew the feeling. "Whatever it is, you can talk to me. With the last several turns I've had, I don't think I can be surprised by much. And, as for Yorm's concerns, you don't have to worry. I've been caught up in some politics, it seems. I'm working on it."

Zael nodded. "I'm sure you are. You were . . . always good to talk to." Dime waited, and Zael's next words were shaky. "I don't know if I'll make it."

"I'm sorry." Dime didn't know what else to say.

"The medics keep telling me to focus, that healing comes from inside, that if I focus, I can drive out whatever is trying to tear me apart. They say it with big smiles and confident nods. So, what, if I think I'm getting worse, have I not done enough? It's my fault? How do I face Yorm with that on my mind?

"Then my friends come to see me, and they say the same—you'll be fine, you're strong, you can do this." He ran a hand down the side of his face. "I'm not fine, and I'm not doing it. Does that make me not strong?"

Zael accelerated his speech. "So, what am I supposed to do? If I 'think positive,' like they keep saying, maybe I'll return to Sol anyway. Without preparing for it. Before I've made that peace or said what I need to say. Maybe I'll spend my last days feeling like a failure for not doing enough to save myself. But if I let go and . . . allow myself to think what I'm thinking . . . then maybe I'm giving up. Giving up on Yorm, on our children and their children. Or worse, I contributed to my own failure by not trying hard enough, like they tell me to do. It could be my fault." His face was drawn. "What do I do?"

"I don't know." Dime didn't. She wished she had a better answer for her friend. "Maybe take a step back. Think about what feels right. What you'd like to do."

"I can't deal with Yorm being alone at this age."

"That can't be your burden." This was easy for Dime to say, but she knew the dangers of compounded grief in cases of shared misfortune. "Sure, feel bad about it. But don't let it drive your thoughts. Besides, your children won't let her be alone."

Zael burst into a wheezy laugh. A stride later, Yorm's face poked in.

"I'm fine, love," Zael said. "We're just talking."

She closed the door again.

"I'm sorry; that was funny?"

"It was." Zael grinned. "All these last days, and you're the first pyr who's told me to feel bad."

"No, I didn't mean you should feel bad." Had she said that?

He waved off the comment. Dime wasn't seeing any humor in this, but she was glad Zael was amused. He'd always been sort of quirky; she liked that about him. She wished she could stay here longer, share some laughs. They could both use them. But the urgency of getting downcity weighed on her. She reminded herself she'd been seen. Several times.

"So what are you doing?" he asked. She was glad he didn't seem to sense her worry. "Did the fairies really come and take you away?" Instead of showing fear, Zael's eyes lit up, like he was ready for a good story. Now, Dime almost laughed.

"They tried to. I almost met Sol myself; fell off the Great Cliff." Dime tried not to react to Zael's mild gape. "Made my way back to Sol's Reach, healed up, then went back again to find them." She leaned forward. "Zael, I went to their city and confronted their version of the Light. They call him the High Seat. I may have over-stayed my welcome."

He shook his head. "They are *not* going to see you coming."

Dime took the general sense of the compliment, but didn't know what he expected her to do. Outside the window, the bells sounded through the towers. They paused until they stopped.

"I don't know when I'll be back," she said. "I've been seen in the city, so it's only a matter of time until someone gets serious about it."

Other than the thinness of his face, Zael looked much as he always had, the same diligent scholar Dime knew. This comforted her.

He sat up straighter. "Did you ever consider why there are no texts from the Great War? No records of the Fo-ror?" Dime was surprised to hear him use the proper term, though it was familiar to her now. She remembered Rock's story about the fairy storybook that an agent thought ve'd burned.

"I didn't consider it enough," she answered. "It's the sort of thing I think about all the time, now. Not the irony of the IC with-holding facts that might change pyrsi's minds; I'm over my shock at that. But learning what some of those secrets are. And deciding what I'm supposed to do about them. The fairies wanted me, not you. Not Yorm. So, is it my choice to try and help? Or, now, is it my obligation?"

"*Hmm.* What was it you told me? Think about what feels right, what you want to do?"

Dime smiled. "Maybe it's that simple."

"Maybe it is." Their eyes met, and Dime wished she could stay longer. But the risk was too high.

"I have to go. I'm sorry. I'm really happy to see you."

Zael reached a hand out over the blanket and Dime rested hers on it. "I need you to know something," he said. "If I don't make it." He paused, as though Dime were going to argue.

Am I supposed to argue?

"If I don't make it, I want you to know that whatever happens, I'll be proud of you. The Light doesn't control you. The Seat doesn't control you. Your *heart* controls you." He took a long breath. "It was nice to see you. I'm glad you stopped in."

Tears started to work their way up Dime's throat, and intuition told her it wasn't the right time for Zael to see them. Settling her backpack onto her shoulders, she gave him a nod, then turned back out the door. Yorm walked her through the hallway, her smile still uneasy.

"I know it's a lot." Dime said. "He's a good pyr. Always was. And it was good to see you."

Yorm nodded curtly, and Dime let herself out.

A rare rain had broken over Lodon when Dime stepped back onto the street. Her gut felt tight again, both at her sadness over Zael's condition, but also with dread for these next two visits, to the only two victims she could locate in the records. She still felt she had to tell them, especially if they might be in danger.

The two addresses were a ways downcity, but she trudged at least a few rings lower before hailing a car. She was glad to see it had a privacy shield.

She gave the driver her destination neighborhood and slid into the back seat, hoping the driver hadn't had time to recognize her or recall the description of the suspicious former agent. The thought of using one of her signed paynotes crossed her mind, but with her identity tied to the note, she couldn't risk xem getting a hemsa for not reporting her, or for not being observant enough to recognize the wanted pyr.

So she worked one of the smaller notes Ella had given her out of her pouch. It was enough more than the fee to form a generous tip. "Drop me off anywhere here," she said, passing xem the note through the screen as the car stopped, and then leaving before xe could see her face.

The first address wasn't far away. And the rain turned out to be a great help. Although it created a chill on her skin, it kept pyrsi from looking up as they walked.

Until she entered the pyr's tower, no one saw her at all. Her own trepidation grew. Even though her churning gut told her she needed to warn these pyrsi, she couldn't imagine how they'd react. She didn't want to bring them the news. It shouldn't be her burden.

The tower was not a nice one. The walls were musty and out of repair, as if Maintenance had not been called for a while. No one greeted each other, and she passed without note to the sixth floor, where the records indicated he lived.

Fearing she'd lose her courage if she thought a stride longer, Dime knocked on the door. An older pyr, likely in xyr Eroh, answered, not saying anything in response, and wearing disheveled clothes.

"Hello, is Kolk here? I need to talk to him."

The elderly pyr raised xyr eyebrows, then shrugged. "Back there." Xe pointed toward a door. "He doesn't talk, in case you don't know."

Dime walked through, not expecting to be sent unescorted into someone's home. "Hello? Kolk?" The pyr had said he didn't talk.

A pyr sat on a couch, writing or maybe drawing in a wide note-book. Piles of paper littered the room, some with spare garments strewn over them. His eyes widened when she rapped at the side of the doorway. "Kolk? I need to talk to you. May I close this?"

Kolk half-shrugged. Dime had no idea whether that was supposed to be a yes, but with the older pyr looming behind and no direct signs of discomfort from Kolk, Dime went ahead and closed the door. In some sense, the strange visit reminded her of her interviews in the field. She settled into that familiarity as best she could.

"I'm sorry to bother you. My name is Fe'Dime. I'm the pyr in the *Caller*, if you've seen it." Kolk didn't react. "I have information I think you need to know. It's difficult news, if I've found the right pyr."

Dime chastised her own insensitivity; she knew there ought to be a better introduction to this sort of intrusion. But she had no idea how to react to Kolk, or how to read his muted responses, and she wasn't just going to stand here and chatter at him. His level of understanding or consent was unclear. She didn't know what to do.

"Are there . . . scars on your back?" Kolk stopped writing, and his eyes stopped in place. Then, he understood her. He didn't answer. She wasn't going to ask him to look, not like this.

"If you don't want me to continue, please let me know."

Kolk just stared at her. She gathered her nerves.

"You may have heard that I was visited by fairies. That's true. I even went to their homeland. We call it the Undergrowth, but they call it the Heartland." Kolk was still staring, so she went on. "It is . . . beautiful. Tall trees, winding paths, and color and sparkle in every direction."

Dime wished Luja were here to help her interpret Kolk's reactions, to give her a sense of his diagnosis, if there was something affecting him. It wasn't that she wanted to pry; she didn't know how to best communicate with him. Was he simply not talking, or did he have challenges she could accommodate? In some regard, there was an air of depression around him. She hoped it wasn't that; Dime had struggled with depression over the cycles, and she knew its effects. She also didn't want to make his situation worse.

She thought about calling in his homemate, but that didn't seem right. If Kolk couldn't speak, or didn't speak, he could use his notebook. If he was choosing not to communicate, that was his choice.

"If you have the scars, then I believe you were born in the Heartland." She paused, but Kolk didn't look surprised or upset. He was listening intently now. "And if so, your body is Fo-ror. They removed your wings, so you couldn't perform valence and would pass as Ja-lal. They wanted to use you someday, to help learn about the Ja-lal. Maybe . . . to help overtake Sol's Reach. It was a violation, of course."

His flat reactions bothered her more than any type of overt shock or dismay. Dime never dealt well with uncertainty, and she had no idea what sort of an impact she was having on the pyr. "Your body—if you have the scars, you probably have a Fo-ror body. Your healing would not be as fast as a Ja-lal, while your sight in the dark would be better. There could be other differences too. Do you . . . do you understand?"

Even in Kolk's dry stare, Dime knew that he understood. She *sensed* it. The pen rested in his hand. Then, whether he didn't want to respond or couldn't, she would not stay.

"You could be in danger. I don't know. They might come here for you. They might not. They believe in . . . holding pyrsi. Against their will. I'm sorry to tell you this way, or at all, but I thought you'd choose to know. The Fo-ror who did it . . . his name is Ma'Neimano. I'll leave you alone now. If you ever want to talk, send word to the Free Winds, and I'll come back. I . . . wish you well."

Overwhelmed by the confusing visit and the potential harm she might have done, she got up, walked past Kolk and out to where his homemate waited, and with neither of them trying to stop her, she left the small home, rushing down the stairs and then gasping as she spilled out onto the street.

She didn't worry who saw her or not, this time. She continued toward her next stop, trying to get there before she could change her mind. Wiping the raindrops from the top of her head, she stopped for a stride, surprised that again the stubble was growing back, poking through her skin. But of course it was; she'd shaved at Ella's but not since. Not regularly as all Ja-lal did. As she always had.

One foot in front of the other, Dime reached the next address, surprised to see she'd entered a neighborhood of private homes, separate structures not part of the network of towers. Private homes were rare in Lodon, though common outside it. Many of the city's high-class lived in the tall residential towers upcity. The ones with private homes were usually in Nor Lodon, their cabins or mansions built into the climbing foothills.

These homes were perhaps a compromise: a way to work midcity without the longer travel from the nor, or the bustle of tower life. An expensive compromise, as each took the same land as a small tower. Nafat's papers had said he was part of a wealthy high-class family, that he worked at a museum. Trying not to hope that's where he was now, she knocked at the door. A pyr opened it, dressed in a long blue tunic lined with plain lace.

"My greetings. I'm looking for Nafat," Dime said.

This pyr, who Dime took to be a home employee, led her in and showed her to a sitting room, circled with bright lamps and filled with small, elegant tables and luxurious upholstery. Knowing she was wet with rainwater, Dime didn't want to mar the unblemished fabric, and so she remained standing.

Soon after, a pyr strolled into the room, dressed in a fine corduroy suit with maroon ruffles and gold buttons. A folded handkerchief protruded neatly from a pocket, geometric embroidery on its edge. Nothing about xem indicated interest in seeing a visitor.

Xe scanned her face, taking in her tattoos in a most unsubtle way, before breaking into a delighted gasp. "You're that agent everyone is talking about! Agent Diamond! Come in, come in."

"I'm looking for Nafat," Dime repeated. "Please, just Fe'Dime. And I'm no longer an agent."

"Yes, yes, I'm Ma'Nafat. Now please, sit here."

Dime tried to explain that her clothing was damp, but at his continued insistence, she set her backpack aside and sat onto a seat so cushiony, she struggled to regain any sense of dignity as it bounced her around.

Nafat rushed from the room with almost a dance to his step.

Before long, he'd returned, and a new pyr had set a whole tray of pastries, olives, and herbed nut spreads before them, accompanied by a plate of tiny sandwiches: seared dein patties pressed between tiny buns. "Would you like any brew? Or tea?" the pyr asked.

At this point Dime would have taken a shot of ferm, but she wasn't going to say that. "Just some water would be nice." Xe returned with two cups, and then left.

Dime watched Nafat, perched on the thin edge of a plushy sofa. She dreaded telling him her news but she also had no desire to stay and banter here, with her family so close by. "Have one of the sliders, please, before they get cold!" Nafat didn't wait, grabbing a sandwich and pressing the soft bread between his fingers as he took a bite.

He pointed down intently at the tray with his other hand. With a nod, she bit into one of the sliders. The dein patty was nicely warmed, and both crunched and mushed in her mouth. A creamy nut spread complemented a crisp cracker, topped with a scoop of salted beads. *Ok, that is good.* She tried another, this time with a marinated pepper.

But this wasn't why she was here. She reached for a napkin to wipe her fingers. "I'm so sorry to intrude this way, but I have something serious I need to tell you."

Nafat clapped his hands together, bouncing on the seat and rushing to chew the rest of his bite. He waggled the partially-eaten slider in his fingers. "Did you really see the fairies? You're the most famous pyr in Lodon now; do you know that? Everyone is looking for you. So, did you see them?"

Dime's smile was passably polite and the trepidation she'd felt at disrupting this pyr's night eased a touch. "Yes, I did. They came to my home, as has been reported, and tried to take me with them. I was put in great danger that day, which is why I'm here. I need to warn you."

"Me?" Nafat scrunched his nose. "Is this about the museum? Is there something they're trying to *steal*?"

She knew the flippant connection of the fairies to the Violence, even in the form of stealing, wouldn't have bothered her before this began. It bothered her now. Yet, it was hard to lecture him on the general goodness of fairies with the news she was about to deliver.

"It's about you, directly. Or it may be." She made herself ask him. "Is there anything unusual about your back? In the shoulder area?"

Nafat's grin disappeared, and he squinted, concerned. He started to prepare another cracker, then stopped, setting the spreader down. "I'd like to know what this is about first."

As reasonable as that sounded, and considering he hadn't said there wasn't, Dime still wasn't going to disclose the fact of Project Diamondsong to anyone she didn't feel certain was affected. She'd felt certain with Kolk. She didn't need to see the scars to sense them. There had been a connection there, one she'd not understood. A strong sense.

"I can't tell you unless I can be sure." When Nafat didn't respond, Dime stood, reaching for her bag. "I'm sorry to have bothered you. Perhaps I'm in the wrong place." It was admittedly a bluff, but time was continuing to pass, and she was not yet with her family.

"I'm sorry. There is—on my back. But, I'm embarrassed by it; I was in an accident as a ba'pyr, my parther forbid me to tell anyone. I promised ver."

Dime drew in a short breath. She tried to imagine she was looking across at a Fo-ror, but all she saw was another pyr. Quite well-dressed, and now tapping his fingers in concern.

"Then don't tell me about the accident," she offered. "Look. It's your choice whether to know. I'm here to warn you of danger you might be in. If you choose not to hear more, just know that the fairies might try to take you as well." She noted that he perked back up at this, and she shook her head. "No. You would not enjoy their accommodations. And I need to warn you, they hold pyrsi against their will." That dampened his expression a touch. "Burge, you know that pyrsi are looking for me. I need to go. Do you want me to tell you?"

Nafat peeled back his thick jacket, turning his back to Dime. "You may look," he said. "But I don't know why this is relevant."

"I'll have to lift it up." Dime lifted the soft shirt, trying not to touch Nafat's skin out of respect. His tattoos, an array of finely drawn cut gemstones intertwined with wide flourishes, concealed any sign of skin damage. "May I touch?" she asked. "I promise, there's a reason."

"Yes," he murmured, hesitantly.

Uncomfortable, Dime ran her hands over the expert ink, where she thought the scars should be. In those exact places, she felt the texture of the skin change. They were softer than Dime's own scars, but she could feel the two lines, just at the juncture of where she now understood wings to form.

She lowered the shirt. "I'm sorry, but I had to know. Please, put your jacket back on and sit down."

Nafat fumbled with his buttons. "Could you help me?"

Dime tried not to show any reaction as she reached toward him, fastening each gold button. "Please brace yourself." Nafat nodded, biting his lip. Dime took a breath. "Biologically, you are a Fo-ror. A fairy. Your wings were removed to place you here, when you were a ba'pyr, as a hidden agent to be used against our kind if needed."

Nafat rose, his fingers over his mouth and eyes growing wide. "Really? *Really?* That's . . . amazing."

Dime couldn't believe what she was hearing. As Nafat began to list off all the things he surmised about fairies, and how excited he was for this news, Dime felt a sudden fear. It wasn't her choice whether to keep his secret, but she wasn't sure it was in anyone's interest for him to tell it further. She hoped that was her reason, rather than knowing that Nafat telling his story could reveal hers.

"Nafat. You should consider whether it's wise to tell anyone. For now. You saw the way pyrsi reacted to the fairies. Pyrsi are on edge. I . . . look, it's your choice, but telling pyrsi now might put others in danger."

Nafat didn't seem like he'd want to endanger others. Again, he bit his lip. "I won't tell. For a while. Are we going home? Are we going to go find them?"

We? Had he already made that connection or was she reading into his words? Dime hadn't said she was like him also. But, wouldn't that be implied? *Holy harm.* "I, uh," Dime had felt connected to these victims, but it jarred her that she didn't know this pyr at all. She didn't want him making assumptions about her, and she didn't want to address them.

She'd delivered her warning; now she wanted to get to her family. She'd been in town, she'd been seen, she needed to go.

"I'm sorry—I have things I need to take care of. I have to go for now. Please, remember what's at stake. The fairies being seen here, especially if it happens again, could push pyrsi back to confrontation between the two societies. We can't let that happen, and it's still all new and confusing. If I were you, I'd take some time and try to understand what this means. Maybe get out of here a while." She glanced around the lamplit room. "That's what I intend to do."

"But I want to help." Nafat stood, his hands clasped together.

Dime wished she could tell him how. But she didn't know. Except, in some ways she did. "Something I've learned—"

He nodded, urging her to continue.

"Our prejudices toward the Fo-ror are so prevalent in even small actions and words. They are also based primarily on untruth. If you want to help, start by changing those perceptions. Help me spread the word that pyrsi should not believe what they hear. That the fairies—no, call them Fo-ror—are not inherently bad, no more than we are."

Nafat was muttering to himself. "Ways to help . . . sure, I can think about that."

"I'm sorry to deliver the news so abruptly, but I need to go."

"Yes, of course—and I may call you Dime?"

"Yes, please."

Dime walked back out toward the front door, Nafat at her side. He rushed ahead to get the door, and thanking him, she stepped through.

Now, to find her family. She glanced around, glad to see it was no longer raining, but then jumped, seeing Nafat had followed her onto the walk. "You really don't want to be seen with me," she cautioned.

"No, it's fine. Here, I'll accompany you."

No time for this. "It was really nice to meet you and I'm sure we'll talk again, but I have something important I need to do right now. And I need to be alone." Dime felt that was true. If Ador was keeping her family in hiding, she'd want his permission to reveal where.

"Oh, ok. But I'll see you again?"

Dimly, she acknowledged she'd sought a connection with these pyrsi, maybe someone who understood. Instead, they were strangers who felt distant. Uncomfortable. Still, maybe one of these days she'd want to share experiences, and right now, Nafat was her best option. "Sure, that'd be great," she said with a polite smile.

It took a little extracting for Dime to move away, walking faster when she felt certain that he was not behind her.

So much of the night had passed, and Dime wasn't sure what good she'd done. She was glad to have visited Da-da and Zael, and seeing Batu was great, but she hadn't been able to discuss events with Ador. Kolk's situation had confused and troubled her, and Nafat had seemed almost *excited* by the news, though that was probably an early stage of denial.

At least she had the map to the den. And she was almost to her family now. Almost there. They could get out of the city and plan their next steps. Though, the pain in her gut reminded her, she was only one pyr and she had no idea what the next event would be. What could she ever do?

Dime's spirit was littered with emptiness and confusion.

And so she hastened her steps, trying not to draw attention as she neared the location Dayn had indicated, a market district dome where they sometimes met to play cards. The small, somewhat rundown building was awkwardly positioned between a main street and a diagonal alley, almost lost between the taller buildings surrounding it.

She stopped, noting that even after the rain, the midcity streets were bustling again. Nearing the market's edge, she saw a stack of the *Caller*.

RUMORS ABOUT INVADERS FADE
Missing Agent Suspected Behind Hoax

Hoax?

She couldn't be seen here, not with her family so close. Knowing she'd look rude but hopefully not recognizable, Dime swept up a copy, opened it wide, and held it in front of her face as if too engrossed to put it down while walking. Finding a clear path, she tromped across the street, holding the paper like a mining shield until she reached the dome and walked in. She backed up against a side wall and peered around the paper, but only saw a few strangers, seated around a worn table.

"Here," a voice whispered, stepping right in front of Dime to block her from view. She didn't recognize the pyr, but xe ushered her behind a set of shelves, leading her to a plain door. It looked like a storage closet, but inside, she saw a set of stairs.

She ran up them, bursting into the room where Tum was lounging on a bed, Dayn was seated at a table, and *whoosh*—

Luja slammed into her like a windstorm, wrapping vis arms around her and choking back sobs, or laughs, maybe. Dime curled her arms around her child, rocking ver back and forth as they stood. It took some effort to pry herself back and look into Luja's eyes, especially now that her own were clouded with tears.

"Ma-ma," Tum's voice cried from the bed, little Agni cuddled in her arms. Dime rushed over and sat next to her, pulling the ch'pyr close and covering her tear-covered face in kisses. Agni mewed and then jumped down to the floor with a thud and a squeak.

Luja joined them on the bed and threw vis arms around both of them. Together, they held each other and cried, and Dime stopped thinking about anything else.

Dime was finally allowed to stand, and she turned back toward that table, a weight both lifted from and pulled at her heart, to see her spouse, her best friend, her *world*, with red eyes and a quivering smile.

"Hey," he said.

Swinging the heavy backpack down next to the bed, she no less than bounded toward him, pressing her face against his and not attempting to stop the tears that continued to flow. His strong shoulders, his smooth face, his bony hands, she sunk into all of it.

Finally she stepped back, all of them sniffling. And—if Dayn's button wasn't still loose on his jacket. She flicked it with a finger. "I was just saying, we need to tighten this back on. You wore it like this—this whole time?"

"Did you really fall off the Great Cliff, escape the Undergrowth, then go back on purpose?" By his expression, he seemed unsure whether he was upset by this or impressed.

"That— Well, yes, I did. Except I don't call it the Undergrowth anymore. It's the Heartland, the home of the Fo-ror. And it's nothing like what we've been told."

A knot grew in her chest at the thought of telling them her biggest news. She thought it would've been a relief, but now, seeing their tear-streaked and pained faces, how could she add this? She had to. Her next question allowed her to stall, just a while more. Tum was bouncing on the bed, and Luja was tearfully sipping down a cup of water. She lowered her voice, talking now only to Dayn.

"This is a Free Winds . . . secret home, then?" She almost said meeting place, but it looked more like a residence. And she could have said den, but even now, she couldn't get past the idea of a non-IC hiding place. She'd unpack that later.

"It is. They let pyrsi live here sometimes who don't want the Circles knowing they're in town, I guess. Ador wasn't too specific about it. He apologized earlier when he stopped by, for being so vague. Said he's getting used to the idea of me being wrapped up in this."

He's going to have to get used to more than that, Dime thought.

"These Free Winds are an odd lot. I'm sure that sounds

ungrateful; don't take it that way. It's more of an affiliation, hard to even call it an organization. I never know who's involved or who will be around. I'm not here to defend the Circles, but with all their process, leadership at least knows who they're dealing with. The Free Winds are—"

"Too free?" Dime offered with a grin. They both laughed.

"When your friend came by, she suggested it might be best to stay out of sight until we better understood what had happened. She said you were working on it." Dayn smiled. "I went to talk it over with Ador, though I didn't tell him who had suggested it, and he immediately offered this place."

Dime wasn't sure how she felt about staying in what appeared to be an outlaw refuge, though, she supposed after barreling out of the complex, she was two strides from being one herself.

"I hope you can talk to him soon; he's been so worried about you," Dayn continued. "It really rattled him that he'd just stopped by before they arrived. He kept saying if he would have stayed, maybe he could have helped."

"Helped with what?" It was so like Ador to take on other pyrsi's burdens. "If he were there, would we have done something different?" Dime didn't even like thinking about it.

At the time the pyrsi had burst through her door, she'd been so scared by their conduct and so unsure of their ethics, she'd just wanted to get away. During her subsequent time with the newts, she'd worried over and over again whether she should have stayed and tried to talk to them. Or just . . . told them to leave, the way Suzanne had with the Light. Perhaps she'd been wrong to put others in danger, running through the city.

But now, after learning of Neimano's plan, she was glad she'd gotten away. The High Guards had been there on orders; they wouldn't have had the authority to reason with her. They could have, of course, but they wouldn't have thought of it that way. Even if her leaving had started a bit of an avalanche, she didn't regret it now.

As if reading her thoughts, Dayn nodded. "I don't know what we could have done, either. It's easier to plot it out when you're not in the middle of it. It's different there, in the moment, with no context. Anyway, I've actually thought they did see him leaving. They probably thought he was me, and that's why they went in. They thought you were alone."

That made sense. "We need to talk to him," Dime agreed. "Problem is, I don't think we can wait here."

Dayn responded with raised brows.

"I uh, ran a few errands. And . . . was seen at the complex. Also, there's a lot more going on. I've learned some of it, and, uh, I'd like to get everyone out of the city as soon as possible." Though their voices were still lowered, Dime could see Luja and Tum intensely acting like they were not listening.

Seeing the same thing, Dayn lowered his voice further. "Let me pull our things together. Let's give them a stride to adjust."

It warmed her the way Dayn immediately trusted her and knew explanations could come later. "Agreed." Dime stalled again with her larger news, preferring to hold her children again before they set out.

She sat back down next to Tum, who rolled over and snuggled against her side. Dime wrapped an arm around her, giving her a few squeezes. She grinned at Luja from the other side. "I could have used you when I fell off that cliff." Rolling up the sleeve of her tunic, she held her arm forward.

"Ma-ma!" Luja took Dime's arm and rubbed vis hand along it. "That's a bad scar; you must not have been able to treat it for a while."

"I did my best."

"Ma-ma," Tum said. Dime turned her head. "What are the fairies like?"

"They're mostly like us, Tum." The knot grew. She had to tell them. But Dime really wanted to get out of here. Dayn was moving efficiently around the room, packing their bags; he might be done any stride. Yes, she'd tell them everything at the den. "I want to get out of the city for a while, and then we'll discuss all of it. Ok?"

"It may be complicated to get out without being seen." Dayn

walked over, slinging a tied bag onto the floor. "Ador has a toothcar we can use, but all cars leaving get a full inspection at any gate."

She noticed he wasn't hiding any of this from Tum and Luja. Well, they saw him packing.

"By car or by foot," he'd continued, "the Circles aren't going to like you being out in public, especially without knowing what you know. They may ask you to come back for questioning. If you do, well, we're all right in the middle then. If you don't, you'll be an official outlaw, on the public bad side of the Circles. Either . . . would be a big step."

Sometimes Dayn stated the obvious. And she'd *promised* herself she'd take a toothcar this time. But he was right. Even if Dime could slip out, four pyrsi, four bags, a wheelchair, and a kita would be much less subtle.

"I've already been seen; pyrsi will be searching for me soon if they aren't now. And I agree—I can't let the Circles call me in. Not yet. The situation is complicated, and I haven't had time to consider everything I've learned here. But I just can't be where pyrsi can find me until I've had time to sort it out. We need to go."

She glanced up at Dayn, not sure whether she was being too forceful. It wasn't only her choice.

He looked like he wanted to ask her something, but his eyes rested on Tum and Luja. Across the room, Agni was crouched under a table, glaring at all of them. Dime let go of Tum and stood up, walking over to Dayn.

"We're still here," Luja said.

"I'm allowed to talk to your father in private. And there's"—she waved around—"only one room, and I'm not going to talk to him in the bath." She lowered her voice. "What is it?" she asked Dayn.

"Do you really think they would do something to you? The Circles? Remember, Dime, I have no idea what you've seen or been through. We were home, scared, for four turns. Now all I know is that the, uh, witch of the woods visited me, acted quite non-witchy, and told me to get out of sight. So, now we've been here for the last four. It's been a little stressful. Do you know more? Is . . . the Violence an issue?"

All of these questions were loaded.

"I don't know. It's possible." She felt a twitch in her back. "First, don't call her that; it's a terrible story. Second, I need to get away until we can talk through it all—what I learned in Pito and what I learned tonight—and decide what to do. I really want to get out of here. Just for a while."

"There's more?"

Dime nodded. Dayn reached forward and pulled her into a long hug. Agni let a warbling cry and ran, jumping back onto the bed. Standing tall, she continued to mew.

Unsure what was bothering the kita so much, Dime glanced around the room. Everyone now held still and quiet, and Dime thought she heard a ringing noise. "What's that?" she asked, peering across the room to a few small, dingy windows. She walked over, Dayn following.

"Harm," Dayn muttered. A group had formed on the street below, gathering under a large lamp. One pyr at the group's edge was clanging old metal pipes together and shouting something.

"Game night starting soon?" She attempted a weak smile.

"No. And you are one magnet these days." He tried to smile back. "I'm so sorry. Whatever it is."

They'd have time to discuss that later. "Look." Taking a step back, Dime pointed to a pyr below, wearing an embroidered Sol's Pillars insignia over xyr jacket. "Can we go now?"

"Yeah, I'm with you." He turned back. "Hey, kids, we're going to go right now rather than wait. Can you get your things? Don't take time for anything that isn't important." Dayn pushed Tum's chair next to the bed. Tum reached over and swung herself into it, clipping her straps into place. Tum called over to Luja, who pushed a couple of items into Tum's bag and handed it to her.

"We stayed mostly packed," Dayn said. "Without knowing much, I didn't want to get too comfortable." He glanced at Luja, who was rushing to tie vis bag. "It's been strange for us here. Seeing what the fairies did shattered my view of everything. We were left uncertain, scared. Those first four turns, not even knowing whether you were well. What they were doing to you. And then we moved here, forced to stay in one room, watching every noise we made, without any sense of how long we'd stay. The Violence wasn't even part of our *lives*, Dime. And now we've been hiding in its shadow."

He didn't lower his voice. The kids, of course, they knew. They'd been through all of it.

"Done," Luja called.

Dime peered through the window, trying not to get too close. "There's more now. *Harm it.* Someone must have followed me." She didn't even consider the possibility of a coincidence. Sol's Pillars had found her, and . . . she knew they were here for her. Like at the gates. They weren't going to stop. They weren't going back into the corners.

There was an *obsession* to it.

"Dayn, whatever happens out there, I want to stick to the plan. I want to get us out of here and get to the den. I have a map. First, we have to leave the city and not be followed. Ugh, how did they know I was here?" She hadn't been careful enough, but *harm it all*, this was her city, and she hated all this sneaking and moving.

The image of Neimano's cage flashed in her mind, and she tried to push it away. She wasn't going to let him find out where she was, or where her children were. If she had to keep moving, then so be it. They'd need to stay sharper. Dime wasn't used to this idea of real danger, but she'd better get used to it. For now.

"Any tricks to getting out?" Assuming there was no secret passage, she wasn't sure what he'd have to offer, but the crowd below was unnerving her. How could they just walk into it?

"Like last time, I suppose. We just go."

Interlude

The note from Paminila had been unexpected, and Jinnili was filled with worry.

He'd been too forward at the garden, and he'd spent the last turn worrying that he'd ruined their friendship. He hadn't meant to be rude; the invitation had popped out of a hidden place inside him, but she'd flown away before he could take it back.

Worry clouded his thoughts. He'd skipped the last daylight shift in his fear. Maybe they'd think him ill. Maybe he was. He was afraid to face her. Just until he could find a way to reset. To put things back the way they were.

There was nothing he dreaded more than the idea of losing Paminila's friendship. Seeing her at the gardens was the highlight of each shift. The spans away from her were flat, plodding. Their conversations, her smile, they brightened each take together.

Then he'd received the note, asking if he'd meet her and signed . . . *Paminila.*

The note led him to a huge tree, the sort with swinging gazebos and private decks. She was low class, like him, just a worker—surely she wasn't in a fine place like this.

He flew upward, looking for the sign indicated on the note. He showed it to a pyr sweeping a platform with a broom. "That's all the way up top," xe said, pointing. "Must be a special night." Xe grinned.

"Uh, sure," Jinnili stammered, flying up again.

When he reached the top, the sign indicated he was in the right place. A table was set, only for two, with a single steaming pot on the ledge. Over the top of each plate, little cut violets were arranged in an artful shape. Glowstones were hung from crossing strings, swaying in the night breeze. He glanced around, nervous to be in such a fine tree and thinking he would get into trouble. Surely, they weren't allowed here.

A fluttering of wings interrupted his thoughts, and he jumped, turning around in fright. *Paminila.*

"Um, hi." She wouldn't meet his eyes. "You invited me for pots sometime, but you didn't say where, and I have a friend who works here, and so I brought some food— Would you . . . would you have a meal with me?"

His mouth moved wordlessly, and Paminila grimaced. "I'm sorry, maybe I misunderstood you. I thought you said—"

"No, uh, no, I did, it's just—" He didn't know how he could share pots like this; he'd been hiding his feelings for so long, what if they came out. *My feelings?* He glanced with guilt at Paminila. Maybe she'd heard his thoughts. She was wearing a violet-colored robe, like the flowers on the table. And a little gold pin. He'd never seen her wear a pin before.

"You can go if you'd like. It would be . . . fine."

"No," he said, a little too quickly. "I want to stay."

She scooped a chunky stew onto both plates. "It's not very fancy, but it's a family recipe."

"It smells good," he responded, immediately scolding himself for the terrible response.

A pyr landed on the deck with a carved violin and began to play. Paminila turned aside. "I'm sorry, maybe this is too much."

"I can leave if you want."

She gazed back, her eyes low. "If you want to."

I want to leave? "It's just, I like working with you. We're friends."

"A meal won't make us not friends," she replied. "I'm sorry about the music." She took another bite. "Unless you want to dance."

Dance? Does she WANT to dance? His eyes rested on the glimmering gold pin, then, embarrassed, he looked away, but there was the violinist; he looked at the table.

"If I dance with you, I don't think we can just stay friends." He dropped the spoon, and it clattered in the dish. He rushed to pick it up.

"I could be ok with that."

He forced himself to look in her eyes. *Oh.*

They rose from the table, and she extended her hands. He reached out to grasp them. Her wings began flapping and he tried to match her. At first, they almost tilted over, but as they rose, they found a rhythm.

Together, to the sweet melody of the violin, they twirled through the treetops, above the hanging glowstones, and up past the canopy, where the skystones shone through a thin layer of clouds. Their hands remained clasped.

"May I kiss you?" she asked.

Still in flight, he leaned forward, and their lips locked together. Yearning, he met her warm lips and fell into them. She kissed back, each new kiss pulling him toward her.

Losing balance, they tumbled down, and she gripped his hands tighter as they lowered back to the wood planks below, landing with an uncomfortable bump.

"Sorry," he said, his mind still spinning. "I forgot to fly."

"That's alright," she said, her eyes twinkling. "I didn't let go."

Nervously, they laughed together, with the violin still playing beside them.

"I had one more thing, but it's probably silly." Paminila turned coyly away.

"No, please, show me."

"Ok. Don't laugh." She reached into a little cloth bag and took out a handful of little sparkles. "I ground them myself," she said.

The particles rose from her hands. He could tell she was concentrating, and the little gems began to swirl like a tiny whirlwind, spreading out into the night, surrounding them. From inside, he gazed out at a glitter sky.

"They're like diamonds," he said. Paminila smiled.

He looked into her wide eyes, as the spices from the stew wafted past them and the sparkles flashed behind her.

"I'm sorry," she said. "They were supposed to be while we were dancing. Only if you wanted to dance, of course."

Jinnili wasn't entirely sure what was happening, and he hoped they were still friends. There was only one question left on his mind. "May I kiss you again?"

Act 3

The Gates

Only a narrow flight of stairs led down from the second-floor shelter, so Dayn leaned Tum's chair back and Dime walked backward in front of them, half-carrying, half-bumping Tum down the stairs as Luja followed behind. Tum comforted Agni and let her curl back into her arms. Dime put her hand on the door. Dayn nodded.

The side door where Dime had entered was even narrower than the stairwell, maybe too tight for Tum's chair. So she was alarmed, but not surprised, when Dayn turned around the row of shelves and toward the larger front door, near where the crowd had gathered.

Silently, they walked across the circular room and ignored the murmurs around them as they exited onto the lamplit street. There was no uproar as they passed the gatherers, but a rustle of whispers. Even the clanging sound stopped.

As they walked down the street, with only a few toothcars grinding along in the distance, the crowd began to follow them. Every time she turned around, their numbers had grown in size. Dime didn't know whether they were all there to pursue her, or whether some were just following for curiosity, but her heart pounded with unease, glad they were at least keeping a distance.

Unsure what could happen next, Dime knew her family needed to be told. Finding it harder to say than she'd anticipated, she wrenched every strand of strength from her gut and pushed the words out.

"I have to talk to you," she said through heavy breaths as they moved down the street. "You need to know in case we get split up again."

"We're not getting split up," Dayn murmured.

"I know, but please don't make this harder. I have to tell you what I've learned, and it's hard to say." Her heart pounded; she'd never known words could be so difficult to speak.

"This is strange way to have a talk, Ma-ma," Luja remarked. "Especially with your, uh, entourage back there." Dime would have laughed if the knot within her weren't held so tight.

"It is. Let me finish."

Say it.

She shoved at the words. "When I was a ba'pyr, I was taken from my original parents."

"Taken?" Tum gasped in a half-cry.

"Yes, Tum. A heinous act. Xe or they were told that I died of a disease. I did not die. I was, then, a Fo-ror. A fairy."

Dayn faltered with the chair, and Dime could see him trying to decide if he'd heard her correctly while forcing his expression to hold for her benefit. She wanted to get it all out first, before she addressed Dayn, or thought about the pyrsi following them.

"A pyr had my wings removed with . . . surgery and then flew me to Lodon, where he left me in the Circles' complex, hoping I would land with an important family." She sped her words. "I was supposed to be a secret agent, told someturn who I was so I would act on behalf of the Fo-ror. This wasn't sanctioned; it was a rogue leader who carried this out.

"That's why they came to get me: I quit my career. Maybe they wanted to tell me to go back or maybe they meant to interrogate me. I'm not sure. The pyr who did it is dangerous, and I'm not going to ask him. So, biologically, I'm a fairy without valence. But in all ways, I'm Dime, I'm Ma-ma, and I'm still me. Nothing has changed except what pyrsi might think about me. I needed you to know. Sorry, I should have told you in the room. It was . . . hard."

The exhaustion of having forced the words out flew from her like a small tornado, and she walked along, trying to regain her composure. Behind them, the crowd continued to follow. It grew louder, or perhaps only now Dime allowed herself to hear them.

Her secret spoken, Dime's hands shook and she felt light. It was though a hole had opened in her, for how exposed she felt here, saying the words, worrying her family, all as they walked in uncertainty along the dusty street. Rather than feeling comforted she'd finally released the words, the wound stayed open. Just the pressure was gone.

"We love you, Ma-ma," Luja said. "When we get away, I have some questions." Ve murmured to verself something about physiology.

This calmed her a little. Of course Luja would jump right to the medical implications; vis passion for the career was often consuming. Dime admired it.

"Do you know this is sort of awesome, Ma-ma?" Tum added. Agni squeaked from her lap.

"It's not awesome, Tum, they *stole* her and *hurt* her." Luja sounded angry.

"Not that, obviously. What, do you think I'm terrible? But who else do you know whose mother is a fairy?"

"Well, that *is* pretty cool," Luja conceded.

As they continued to go back and forth bickering in whispers about their fairy parent, Dime looked over at Dayn. "It's true," she whispered. "I'm sorry. If it bothers you that you didn't know, remember I didn't know either. It wasn't a lack of insight. Who would ever think it?"

Dime started to worry at Dayn's lack of response.

"Tum might be right," he said with a forced smile. "Also, your scars— I never even considered— We'll talk about it later. Right now, what should we do? Will they keep following? This is so strange."

It hadn't sunk in yet, but she was grateful he was trying to make this easier. And harm all of this that she couldn't just enjoy seeing him again. Instead, she had to dump this huge secret on him. And in the street. Her stomach churned again. And now they had to focus. *Dayn, we'll figure it out.* The sympathetic eyes he offered her indicated he was thinking similar thoughts.

She glanced again at the crowd behind them. Some were starting to call for them to stop, shouting out that it was her, the fe'pyr who'd brought the fairies. "I say we get a car." Still rattled, she said the first thing she thought. "I am not going all that way again without a car."

"You have enough paynotes to buy a car? Or did you mean rent?"

"Not enough to buy. I have my signed notes left, but I doubt they'll take those." She couldn't imagine who would want to transfer a paynote linked to Dime, at this point. "We'll just hail for now."

"Hail," Dayn repeated. "Who would drive you?"

"Who would drive *you*?" Dime quipped, tense. Paynotes. Toothcars. Thinking back to what Ferala had said, she remembered his dig that Ja-lal would work for payment, no matter the source. It wasn't true, in general. But, pyrsi did like providing for their families. There was nothing wrong in it.

As they moved even further downcity, and the road widened, surrounded by shops designed for visiting villagers, the crowd moved closer, closing the distance between them. "Traitor! Traitor!" one called out, and xyr spark ignited the crowd, as now many were calling and heckling, not just for them to stop, but with names and jeers. Making a decision, Dime turned down a side alley, the type where toothcars would be parked, waiting for fares.

Her family followed, and together they wound around the first few cars, which were empty.

"Hey, there." She waved one of Ella's unsigned paynotes at a waiting car. The driver was leaning against it, and jumped when she drew near.

"I'm the one who was attacked by fairies. I want to get out of the city. If you want me out too, I'd appreciate a ride."

The driver took one look at Dime's distinctive vine tattoos, hopped in xyr car, and pulled off down the alley.

A second car rejected her, then a third, and Dime knew the mob would catch up to them any stride.

The fourth car was willing to take them—an Aoch driver who probably wanted a story to tell xyr friends. Dime didn't want to endanger someone so young, and started to turn xem away. They'd just have to keep moving and figure out a new plan.

Luja interrupted, pulling her aside. "Xe's my age, Ma-ma. If I'm old enough to leave the city, xe's old enough to help me. Look, you told xem who you are." Ve pointed over at xem. "Xe's not a ch'pyr; it should be xyr choice." Dime saw the warning signal in Luja's eyes.

"Ok, ok." She leaned in toward the driver, holding two unsigned notes. "I need you to know, you could be in trouble with the Circles or Sol's Pillars over this. Do you still want to help?"

"I don't care about Sol's Pillars. Trash, all of them."

She disliked the harmful language, but the mob was turning the corner behind them. "Alright, but still, be careful. When you get back, you have my permission to tell them you were nervous about saying no to me. Your choice. We want to leave the city, and we're hoping you'll drive us a ways out. I'll pay you more once we're out there."

The youth grinned and snatched both notes into xyr hands. "Get in," xe said. "I know about fairies, anyway," xe added with a lilt.

Dime was unsure whether the enigmatic remark was an empty boast or if it had a story behind it. Behind them, Dime heard the clamor of the crowd, which slowed as pyrsi fed into the alleyway and around the parked cars.

Quickly, they loaded into the Aoch's toothcar, with just enough room for Tum's chair in the back. "I want to stay in," Tum said, which Dime knew to mean she wanted to stay in her chair and not be lifted into one of the car's seats. "In case we have to get out." Dime nodded, wedging her as securely as she could and closing the gate behind her. Agni's fur was puffed out, and Tum petted her, trying to calm the agitated kita.

The pyrsi rushing ahead of the crowd were almost there, and seeing Dime and her family had gotten into a car, someone shouted for them to stop, other calls quickly joining the first.

"Whoo!" the driver hollered, ignoring or perhaps not hearing them, as xe started pedaling down the alley. With the chair and all their bags, the car was groaning and slow. Dayn swung himself over and into the second driver's seat and started to pedal with xem.

"If you don't mind," he said.

Pulling out of the alley, they turned onto another of the large streets leading to the sur end of the city. Dayn and the driver were focused on the view ahead, but Dime twisted around, seeing lines of pyrsi now pouring from the alley's exit and running after them.

The pyrsi tried to keep pace, but after a take they had fallen back, collapsing on the ground in defeat or hunched over, with hands pressed against their thighs. There was no relief in it; Dime knew the most fervent contingent was amassed at the Great Gates, immersed in some rolling vigil or rally or who cared what it was. That group would not be as happy to see her this time.

Though, maybe word hadn't reached the gates that she was in the city. If so, they just needed to outrun the rumor. Except, what had Dayn said? *Inspections.* Toothcar inspections were being conducted at the gates; how were they going to get around that? She wasn't eager to overtly disobey the Circles, and it would be the Enforcement Circle conducting them.

As the gates came into view, Dime leaned forward to Dayn. "I want you to get them out of the city first. I just . . . can't handle it otherwise. Enforcement has my description by now, but it's less likely they're looking for you. Yet. Talk your way through, if you can. Get down the road, and then I'll catch up. Do you agree?"

Dayn thought a stride, his face pinching, then nodded. Whispering a promise that he'd see her soon, Dayn stopped the car. Dime hopped out, walked to the edge of the wide street, and crouched down by the side of a restaurant pavilion. Just above her, she heard casual conversations and the clinking of dishes and utensils. She wished she could be up there, not here in fear and uncertainty. How luxurious normal turns felt now. She crouched, peering out at the promenade ahead.

As the car reached the gates, she wrung her hands and watched as the car stopped for the inspection. She wished she could hear whatever Dayn was telling them, but she was glad it was him there, not her. Dayn was so clever; he'd come up with something. She saw him flash an object, probably his Circles ID, and gesture ahead. The car's teeth again gripped the road, and the toothcar pulled through the gates. Dime exhaled.

Then another officer stepped into the road, pointing out toward the car. Maybe someone had recognized Dayn and realized his association. She needed to draw their attention, to let the car gain distance. Her children could not be part of this.

There were two gambles on the table. First: whether the Sol's Pillars would let her leave, or whether the doctrine preventing the Violence had shattered and it wouldn't be safe to pass through. Second: whether Dime trying to leave could cause that breaking point to occur.

Either way, she couldn't just sit there and worry.

Dime called to the gathered Sol's Pillars supporters as she approached, waving her hands. "Hello! It's me again, Dime." A hush fell, and every pyr within view turned, craning their necks to see if it was really her. With all eyes on her, no one watched the car, cranking away. With her own view clear down the main road, Dime noted the direction it took, watching it turn from the road before disappearing in the darkness.

Dime slowed her steps and tried to project calm, as the Sol's Pillars continued to stare. There was more energy to them than before. Not enthusiasm, but a bottled frustration. It made sense: the attack was a full eight turns ago, and all these days and nights, these same pyrsi had sat here, who knew how many shifts each, boiling in their own fear and rage. And then they'd let Dime walk right through them into the city, which some may have suspected by now. She needed to be careful, but she also needed to leave before she made the situation worse.

The Enforcement officers waited on each side, presuming, she supposed, that she was on her way to talk to them. With as much dignity as she could gather, she held her head high and walked right through the center of the Great Gates.

Quickly, hoping the officers couldn't see her over the crowd, she wove into the ranks of Sol's Pillars, offering greetings as she walked. "Hello, yes, hi. I need to leave; that's what you want, right? I promise I'm leaving now. It's in your best interest not to stop me, right? If you were going to make me leave, then that's taken care of, as I'm leaving now." They seemed to be considering this, as Dime continued to weave through.

"If you want to keep the fairies away, then you need me to leave. They have a thing for me, it seems. Family business, nothing you need to know." She continued talking as the unrest around her grew. "Let everyone know that I've left. Make sure everyone is aware, ok? Thanks."

Dime gasped as she recognized the toothcar returning under the row of tall lamps lining the main road, the same one that had just taken her family through the gates. Peering in the dark, she couldn't see who was still in it. As it drew closer, Dime made out the driver, alone. Xyr face was terrified, and the back gate was open, dragging along the ground. *No.* If xe'd been scared by the implications of driving through the gates, xe just needed to get back inside, before xe said anything about her family. She pled with xem in her mind, *just go. You're fine. Just go.*

"She made me do it!" the driver called. "She made me! Don't convict me, please."

MADE HIM? She'd said he could say he was nervous, not that she'd committed the Violence by coercing him. *No, no, no.*

"She? What do you mean, she?"

"The traitor—that was her family. She was there at first and made me take them. I'm sorry! Her family, they're down there; I escaped them and came back!" Driving through the amassed Sol's Pillars must have rattled xem. She'd *known* xe wasn't reliable.

Dime walked more quickly, now hoping they'd stay focused on the toothcar. They didn't. "She can't leave!" a voice called. Pyrsi followed closer, and she turned around. She could accuse the young driver of lying, but she didn't want to endanger xem further.

"Listen to what you're saying," she tried. "If you want to keep the Violence away, don't start it here! Let me leave. Go back to your homes, and jobs, and friends, and families."

Someone lurched toward her, and another pushed him back with physical contact. Pyrsi were grabbing and pushing at each other now, screaming and shouting at the feel of unfriendly hands against their limbs and chests. *No!* Dime wanted to try and stop them, but her family was waiting. Enforcement started to yell and shout, and in the confusion, Dime ducked down and slipped through. Enforcement would convince them to stop. They would, right?

Thinking of her family, Dime ignored the mélange of calls and shouts behind her, though its anger burned in her ears with every step. She broke into a run, remembering that it was dark and the pyrsi here couldn't see as far. No light. No flying pyrsi. She just needed distance this time. Just enough to be out of sight.

She turned left from the road, as the car had, but at a different angle than she'd seen it go. The crowds behind her, locked in pushing and chaos, didn't realize she'd gone at first. She used their confusion to gain distance, running, practically tumbling, over the long shrubby hill leading down from the city. Once she was far enough away, she cut to the side, back in the direction the car had gone. The hill broke into rockier terrain and she slowed by necessity, stumbling over brush and around clusters of trees. She hoped she hadn't missed them.

As she reached the area where she thought they'd gone, she called Dayn's name, her voice dry and cracking. She almost collapsed with relief when she heard Luja calling her and she stumbled toward vis voice. Finally, she saw their shapes, huddled behind a rock formation.

Dayn was kneeling by Tum's chair, and Tum and Agni were both whimpering, as if in chorus.

"Come, on, let's go," Dime said. Not sure what Dayn was doing, she added, "Everything ok?"

Luja turned with clenched fists. "Xe broke her chair, Ma-ma. Xe said xe would help us, that xe cared about fairies. Xe *lied* to us, Ma-ma. That's the Violence; xe lied. That—*killstroke.*"

"Luja, please." Dime threw a look that silenced the ranting Aoch. She knew how ve felt, though. She turned to Dayn, who held his own flustered reaction to Luja's swearing then shook it aside.

"Our driver had a change of heart," he nearly spat. "Pillars spooked xem. Xe was terrified by the crowds; just lost all sense of reason.

"First xe drove off the road, hoping they couldn't find us. Then, after bumping us over a rough patch to the point I thought we'd tip over, xe demanded we stop, and I couldn't pedal against xem even if I wanted to. Shouted for us to get out, then turned back toward the road. Don't think xe even remembered Tum was in the back; I had to get her out before xe drove off. The wheel bent funny as it caught the cargo rod; now it's loose. I have my tools, but I can't see a thing. Do you have a lamp?"

Dime shook her head. "No, no lamps. Didn't want to carry fuel. I can . . . see a little. Can I look at it?" It wouldn't help; Dime didn't have Dayn's mechanical skills.

Shouts erupted at a distance, and Dime could see faint dots of light spreading out. Dime tried to put aside her memories of the pyrsi shoving each other around. The Violence, erupting. Just because Dime had been there. At least, by the spreading lamps, they didn't know where she and her family were. Maybe she owed the driver that.

"We're actually in danger, aren't we?" Luja asked.

Danger. Why did the word ring a bell? *Danger.*

Dime had promised Ella that if she was in danger near the city, she'd let her know. But Ella was at least two bells away, in her tower. There wasn't time. It didn't matter; Dime didn't break promises.

Hurrying, she wrenched the message flares Ella had made her from the bottom of the bag. She doubted they could be seen from the tower, but even though a glow had started to form on the horizon, it was still dark. Either way, she'd promised.

"Be right back." Sprinting despite her aching legs, she put some distance between herself and her family before jamming the small flare into the ground and lighting it. Though she heard something fly upward, she thought it was a dud. Then, many strides later, as she was running back, a red burst popped high into the air, fizzling and sending a cracking sound echoing through the towers and down the hills.

"What was that?" Dayn sputtered as she stumbled back to him. "Are you trying to bring them to us?"

"Ella. I promised her. They won't see exactly where it came from, but Ella will know we're outside the gates. Or that we were."

"Ella? Is she here?"

"No, but she made me promise."

"You promised to light fireworks when you left the city? Why? Now everyone knows where we are." He stopped. "I'm sorry. It's just—"

"No, I know. I get it. But they already know we're here; the flare doesn't change that. I promised. That's it. Now, I've wasted enough time and we need to get to that den. How do we get out of here?" The mob was moving out from the gates now; from Dime's quick peek over the rock, she could see the glow of their lamps up the hill.

Dayn lowered his voice as she crouched next to him. "The chair's charred bread until I can fix it. Broken, not just loose. I can't repair it here. And she's too big for me to carry now. I would if I could—"

Even behind the large rock, they were too exposed. Dime saw a larger formation at the edge of her vision. "Go over there," Dime said, pointing. "It's more secluded."

With a series of grunts, Dime and Dayn each grabbed a side of the wobbling chair and dragged it, step by step, down a steep hill to an overhang in the small plateau, where they both collapsed.

"I couldn't do that one step further," Dime groaned. "Tum, love, are you ok?"

"I'm sorry this is because of me," she said with a cry.

Dayn swung around in front of her chair. "This is because of a whole lot of pyrsi at this point, none of whom are you. Please, you're my strong buddy, right?"

"I am! I told you, I can just walk. I have my gloves! Let's go."

Dime exchanged glances with Dayn. Tum walked on her hands all the time, but around their home was one thing. All the way across the rocky plains? Gloves weren't enough for that, certainly not for her lower body—they needed to fix the chair. "Tum, you know that's too much. For anyone."

Tum sniffed. "I want us to get away." Dime's heart was breaking inside of her. She didn't think these crowds would harm them, but the uncertainty shook her. She'd seen them pushing each other in fear and discord; maybe that line was broken now. She wished they could just leave.

She went to warn Luja to stay close, but seeing her child huddled under the rock, she knew ve understood.

Dayn continued to fumble with his tools in the dark, trying to feel where the wheel was off and whether he could reconnect it. "It's bent here," he muttered, "so normally I'd have to replace the bar—"

Dime continued to edge to the side of the rocks, looking back up the hill at the moving lights. Absorbed as Dayn was in his diagnosis, Dime didn't want to tell him that the dots of lamplights glowed above them and even past, as the wandering shapes scoured the area. *They know we don't have a car now. They'll keep looking.*

Sol's light grew as well. In the night, she and her family were hidden in the dark shadows. Once dawn arrived, they would be easy to find. There was no time to stay here. Maybe Dime needed to go back, by herself. If she surrendered, they'd stop looking for the others. Dayn wouldn't like it, but—

A familiar bell sounded, faint in the distance. Shocked but understanding, Dime whistled, giving her best impression of a bird that often sat near Ella's kitchen window.

Hoping Ella heard her, Dime repeated the sound in an irregular pattern, finally waving when she saw a familiar silhouette, lampless and stumbling in the low light.

"Here," Dime whispered. "How are you here? Either way, my family's this way." She pointed behind the rock. "We need to get out of town, but Tum's chair is broken. Dayn can't fix it in the dark."

Dayn stood, joining them. His voice was strained. "I don't think I can fix it at all, not without a metal kit."

Ella turned right to Dime, not acknowledging Dayn. "You made quite a scene in the complex, it seems. I had an old friend watching the area; he drove to find me as soon as it happened. We drove back together—you know how I feel about cars—and I've been in the city since, trying to learn where you were. We knew about the midcity mobs, but when I saw the flare, I knew you'd made it out this way.

"Ella! Weren't you worried about being seen, or what the Circles would do?"

"*Bah.* The Circles won't bother me," she growled. "More to lose if they try. Now, we're all in this bucket together." She gave Dayn a nod.

Dayn returned it, then cut Dime a raised brow. "Bucket of pickles," she whispered, still shocked that Ella had found them. "We put ourselves in one."

"Harm's way," Ella agreed. She peered back up the hill, tapping her fingers against her chin.

Dime didn't know what to do either. Maybe she needed to go back and face them, at least for now, then at least Ella could send her word that her family was away. She didn't want to, as she feared they'd make her surrender to Enforcement, but there was no chance she'd let anyone reach her children. The points of light scoured around, their voices getting louder. As was a familiar shuffling sound.

Juni jumped over the rocks, landing right in their midst. Luja screamed from below, following it with another colorful phrase.

Dime raised a hand. "No! No! We're friends! Ella, how the kill is she here?"

"I don't know! They track by scent; I've tried not to think about that. This one came to find me a couple turns back—I call her Juni now too; she said she likes it—Juni tracked me to my tower, I suppose. When I heard you were in the city, I left. I told her to stay there!"

"She didn't!" Dime watched the lights circling closer, wavering as if they'd heard Juni and were searching for the source of the noise. "Everyone! Get out of view!"

They all ducked under the overhang, Juni following. The newt howled at the tilted chair, reaching down and trying to pull Tum into her arms. Dime expected Tum to scream in fear; instead Tum reached back and popped her straps free. The ch'pyr zipped up into the air, cradled in Juni's grip, with the kita still cuddled in her arms. "Hi, Juni, I'm Tum!" she called.

Dime, returning to her vantage point, saw lamps turn and start moving directly toward them, following the sound of Juni's howls. Sol continued to rise, a faint light falling on the terrified faces of Dayn, Ella, and Luja.

"She can't be seen," Ella snapped. "She can't."

Dime agreed. Juni was fast; she could get out before the others had a clear view. But—Tum. No, Dime trusted Juni. She looked at Dayn, "I trust her." Dayn nodded, his eyes wide. He wrenched Tum's bag from the back of her chair and held it out. Juni swept it over her wrist like a bauble.

"Ella, tell her that's my ba'pyr. Take care of her and find us later." Ella started to speak in her form of newt language.

"Tum," Dime got her attention, glad the little fe'pyr seemed more amused by the creature than scared. "This is where we're going." She scrambled to get out the map, and pointed to the den with shaking hands, next showing it to Ella. Ella started speaking to Juni again, appearing frustrated as she tried to think how to describe the den's location. Shouts called over the ledge, and Ella growled out something that was obviously, "Go!"

Juni leapt out onto the plain, Aoch and kita in her arms and bag bouncing beside her, and bounded away just as dawn broke around them, pouring over Lodon's towers and spilling out onto the fields.

"Did you see that?" a voice yelled.

"There they are," another said. "Down there!"

At least a dozen pyrsi closed in, running toward them. Dayn swung his bag higher onto his shoulder. "Let's start walking. These aren't Enforcement. What can they do?"

Dime didn't want to tell him what she'd seen back by the gates: an overt outbreak of the Violence, with pyrsi shoving each other aside in their disagreements. She hoped it was done, knew now the Circles would pretend it had never occurred, that pyrsi involved would never speak of it.

Unless to blame her.

Ella. She had just been through the gates. She must have seen. They shared a glance.

"They could do a lot," Dime said. "Things have changed. Let's try anyway. Luja, stay with us."

They set out, four pyrsi walking together in the light of dawn, walking away from their city and toward the unknown. At first, lamps snuffed one by one, the mob followed behind. Then, others who had been further afield saw the procession and drew toward them, slowly forming a circle, a fence of pyrsi that closed in on them, step by step, and then started moving back in the direction of the gates.

Soon, one of the two groups would be forced to commit the Violence in order to break the other's path, or they would reach a standstill, facing each other until Enforcement arrived to settle the dispute. Which they would quickly, with the aid of toothcars and daylight.

She would do neither. There'd be another way. She'd talk herself through. She could.

Finally, with no way to proceed, they all stopped. Ella was whispering under her breath.

"Look!" a pyr yelled. "The witch of the woods is with them."

Ella actually growled. Dime didn't blame her.

A few pyrsi closed in, towering over them with menacing glares. "You've brought the Violence back!" Their attempt to hold her here was the Violence, she thought. But, she saw, they justified it by the actions they thought she'd taken. Dime did not want to escalate their tensions. She just wanted to leave.

"We've not committed the Violence, and neither will you if you let us pass," Dime said, trying to keep her voice calm, despite a growing fury boiling within her. Images of the High Guards bursting into her home kept flashing in her vision, mingling with these Sol's Pillars, threatening her family, blocking their free passage across open lands. She saw Luja's wide eyes. "Please, just let us leave the city. Isn't that what you want?"

"Leave the city? They're going back to *them!*" Shouts erupted, and calls rang out around the circle. "She's going back to the fairies! She'll betray us!"

"I am not," Dime answered, pushing her fury down further, feeling dizzy now. "I am not going to the fairies. All I am doing is taking my family away from the city, and all I care about is peace and our freedom. Please, let us pass."

Pyrsi threw back conflicting responses, muddling together. Dime saw Ella's eyes were closed, and she was murmuring. Dime had the impression she was trying to decide something. "What?" she whispered.

"They're going to bring the fairies back," pyrsi continued to accuse. "They're going to attack us."

One side of the ring had moved so close to them now that Dime and the others were essentially part of it, facing the way they'd been trying to go. "This is harm," Luja snapped. "Let us through." Ve ducked down, sliding between a gap to pop outside of the circle. A pyr swung around, grabbing Luja's arm. Ve screamed.

Ella and Dayn rushed to Luja as Dime's vision flashed, and the ground cracked under them. Holding each other, everyone scrambled as the land itself opened up into a small, jagged fissure, pushing them upward and away from the others. Ella stumbled, her hands landing on the shaking ground. Dayn's arms wrapped around Luja and they fell back, together, onto the ground. Her stomach lurched.

Most of the pyrsi turned and ran, but the pyr who'd grabbed Luja was standing in the crevice below her, leaning against its side. Xe was howling against the stone as dirt continued to crumble down on xem.

Xyr companions pulled xem onto the opposite side, where the ground had not been raised. Standing, the pyrsi stared upward, across the crevice, at Dime, standing above. "The Violence!" they shouted. "These witches! Kill them!"

Dime didn't know if that was a curse or an actual command at this point, and she felt disoriented, like she was watching a theatrical performance and remarking on the realistic effects. Images flashed: the fairies, the diamond cage, and the pyr with the angry eyes, and xyr hand on Luja, and she followed the coaxing sound of Ella's voice.

A steep hill. Hurry, hurry. Boulders and plateaus and dust and crying. Dime walked and was guided and Sol was bright and the shadows walked in front of her.

"Dime," Dayn's voice cut in. She turned. They were walking, together. "Dime, are you with us?" Luja was crying again. Ella was holding vis hand and rubbing vis arm.

"What happened?" Dime asked.

"I'm not sure," Dayn said, in a low and gentle voice. "The pyr was fine; xe tried to catch us, even. No one was physically harmed, and xe seemed over xyr shock."

Harmed? Dime pictured the landquake and the crack that had opened before them. Xe'd assaulted Luja. That pyr. Had she caused it? No, that wasn't possible.

Dime wasn't ready to talk. The others spoke, she thought, but wasn't sure. Dayn's hand was in hers for a while. That was nice. She squeezed his fingers, and he squeezed hers back.

Using Dime's map, Dayn sent Luja into a village to rent a car. She remembered that. Luja wasn't old enough to rent a car, was ve? Dayn and Luja pedaled the car. Ella and Dime sang songs. That helped. Music was nice. Dime had wanted to leave her career with the Circles and teach music to others. Music helped them. It helped her.

She sang with Ella. Ella's voice was raspy and didn't find the notes, but she liked it anyway. It was wild, like the birds outside her tower. Dime enjoyed listening to her, and she drifted off to sleep, the road bumping underneath.

"Dime, we need to go," Ella said. "We're switching cars." She lifted her backpack up, and walked with them to another car, with Luja as a driver. She didn't think she'd ever seen Luja drive before.

Dime blinked. They were walking again. She said she wouldn't walk out here again. Turning to her side, she saw Dayn, staring at her.

"Hey," he said. "There you are."

"Huh?"

"It's ok. Let's get to the den, then we'll sort it out. Just like you said."

Embarrassment was overtaking her, hardening inside her. She hadn't felt this way since she'd had a bad flu many cycles ago, and a fever that had— This was so embarrassing. She'd lost control, hadn't she? A drug. She'd had a drug.

"Dime, don't worry. Just keep walking."

She was tucked into a bed, and she felt a soft kiss on the side of her face.

Dime sat up and pushed off a blanket. Dayn was there, flossing a thread through his teeth. Blinking, she scanned the room. She recognized what she knew to be one of a few small bedrooms in the IC den. The distant one she'd wanted to reach. As she'd predicted, it was empty. All the agents despised this place.

Besides, Dime felt sure the Circles would not want agents this close to the Heartland until they understood what had happened and what the risks were.

But—it was so far away. They'd traveled so far. How was she here? Events started to blink into place.

"Dayn," she said, but he was already watching her.

"Are you ok?" His eyes held worry.

"I think so." She ran a hand over the top of her head, again surprised by the tiny hairs growing there. She really needed to shave. "I'm so embarrassed."

"There's no need to be embarrassed; you didn't understand what happened either, right?"

What happened.

Dime remembered the pursuers closing in on her and her family. In her mind, she'd repeated that they only needed to leave, that they had to get away from the pyrsi. She couldn't remember much after that, except that a quake had split the rock under them, and they'd been able to get away. A single image returned, of the land pushed up around her, and around her family, and the pyrsi shouting at them from below.

Quakes didn't form underneath pyrsi in distress. Dime knew that. And her own mind was connected to it; she was connected to it. Her mind felt sharp again now, yet unable to cope with all the ideas clamoring for attention.

Settling on one, she thought about the rest of their journey; they'd obviously traveled a long distance. Dime remembered riding in a car. "How did we get cars?" Dime was in no state to lecture, but she hoped they hadn't justified theft.

"A few larger villages offer one-way rentals; it's the same business in both places. I knew that from my own travel, and fortunately that map you got marked which locations did. We sent Luja in—we figured at least no one was out looking for an Aoch yet. Ve did great. Ve's getting to be grown, you know."

Ve was. In fact, Dime knew that the one thing Luja disliked the most was being reminded ve was an Aoch. Vis Bakh was approaching quickly, and Dime didn't know why ve wanted to rush it so much. Old age wasn't really somewhere to rush. She rubbed her forehead.

Dime stood and stretched, walking over to run her hands down the drab walls. "Wallpaper. Only the Circles employ plain wallpaper on purpose. Ugh, this is all coming back now. I disliked this place before. This doesn't help." The décor was probably not her best focus right now. Any worry was best spent figuring out how she'd made a landquake. Perhaps she was avoiding that.

"I'm embarrassed to see the others," she said. She could always be honest to Dayn. That realization comforted her.

"Don't be. Whatever happened, you can say it happened to all of us, alright? Just like the first invasion. We're here together. One team."

Dime turned back and pressed her lips against Dayn's, a sense of self returning, and other feelings too. But her kids were just next door, and— No, not her kids. Luja. Tum was—

"Dayn?" She jumped back. "Did Tum really go with—my friend?" She couldn't bring herself to say the newts until she knew for sure. "Did I dream that?"

"Tum went with Juni, and, I must admit, it rattled my fatherly instinct to let her. But you and Ella seemed confident. Ella told me more about the newts on the way here, how they helped you. They sound nice." Dayn rested a hand on her shoulder. "Is there anything else I need to know? Any unicorns? Dragons? Talking cats?"

That's right, Ella was with them also. *What is a cat?* "I went and saw the fairies, I also stayed a while with the newts, you now know about my birth and biology, and that's it."

"And Ella?"

"She rescued me when I was with the newts. Oh, like I said

before, don't bring the witch thing up again, please. The witch story was spread by the Light because her spouse was a Fo-ror."

Dayn sat back. "Ok, not a witch, but married to a fairy. Ella and I are solid friends now, but that does count for something."

Dime raised an eyebrow.

"Ok, so that's all?" He stared at her intently. "Oh, Diamond, are you ok?"

"I'm fine," she said, sharing one more hug. At least, she wanted to be. She tried to clear her mind as she left to use the bath.

Despite Dayn's reassurances, Dime's nerves caught in her throat as she forced herself to walk into the common area. "Hello," she offered.

Ella was spreading something dark onto pieces of toast, wearing an intent look that didn't soften as Dime greeted her. Luja rested vis elbows onto the table, engrossed in a book. Hearing Dime, ve closed it.

"I'm sorry, Buttons," Dime said. "I didn't want any of this to happen to you or Tum." The guilt of her role in this churned inside. She should have been faster in the city. She should have—

"Ella says Tum is safe with the newts." Luja turned to watch Ella, who didn't react. "I can't stop worrying, though."

"That's natural," Dime said. "But the newts are kind and nurturing, and Tum isn't exactly shy. I'm as sure as I can be that Juni will take good care of her." Dime didn't want to put it this way, but it didn't seem the time to mince words. "We don't know what would have happened with her chair broken as it was. We might be back in the city now."

"With a few hemsa," Luja added. By vis slightly excited tone, Dime did not think ve was taking that seriously enough. "Ma-ma?"

"Yes?" Dime expected more questions about the newts.

"What do fairy wings look like?"

Dime pictured them in her mind. "They are shades of blue, purple, and indigo, sometimes marked with white or silver. They ripple as if the finest fabric could be made of the most elegant stained-glass. The light shines through them, turning daylight into nightlight and nightlight into shimmer." She stopped, unsure what else to say. Ella had looked away.

"I'm sorry they took yours," Luja said.

"It's ok. If they hadn't, I wouldn't have you."

Luja only nodded; ve seemed engrossed in thought. As Dime watched ver, ve looked like ve had something to say, but was still considering it.

They kept mostly quiet as they sat around the table and ate the yeast spread and toast. Dime wanted to talk to Ella without burdening her child further, but knew Luja was sensitive about being left out. She didn't need to worry.

"Can I talk to you?" Ella asked. She turned to Luja. "You'd excuse us, of course?"

"Sure," Luja answered, making verself another slice of toast.

Remembering something, Dime popped back into her own room a moment, searching through her bag. Then she joined Ella in her room.

"This is one dumpy pad," Ella said.

Dime chuckled. "It really is. I didn't want to come back here, but I couldn't think of anywhere else I thought would be empty. And out of view."

"I suppose you realize that occupying Circles' property is against the law."

Dime knew Ella was only saying it to poke at her.

"You told me not to be righteous. Besides, the Circles serve the pyrsi. We're the pyrsi. It all works. Here, I've got something that I owe you."

Dime whisked a bottle from behind her back, the thrill of Ella's reaction eclipsing, for now, her own lingering unease about whatever she'd done outside the city.

"You are bird pooping me on this. This is not what— You tell me. What is it?" Ella couldn't close her mouth in her shock. Dime grinned.

"Here, take it." Dime handed Ella the large bottle. Its charcoal-tinted, expertly shaped glass was set, as if by a jeweler, into a solid gold base, with gold bands climbing and weaving up and around its middle. On top, it was sealed not just with a cork, but with a thick pour of dark green wax, whose dips and drips were frozen into place, like they'd stopped in time.

Ella turned it in her hands, shaking her head.

"And no theft! This is offered compliments of High Seat Ferala, from the Seats' own stock. I have no idea what's in it or what it tastes like, but if it's good enough for the High Seat, then it'll pay a fraction of the debt I owe you."

"Oh, I'd say we're good." She turned her head. "This is really from the Seats' bar. You went to their bar. And got me a ferm." Dime was used to Ella's statements as questions, so she knew no answer was needed. "And you carried it all the way here. For me. *Pffft.*"

Ella sat it down onto the open top of her own large bag, which Dime recognized as the one she'd bought at the Crossing.

"What, we aren't going to split it here? No shared moment?"

"You would have to be kidding me, Burgess Diamond of Ada-ji. This will be enjoyed at the time of my choosing. And probably for no reason at all, because what better way to say you had a ferm from the High Seat than out on the hammock." She turned back to Dime. "Now, this doesn't get you out of any talks we need to have."

Dime frowned. They'd had difficult discussions before; she wasn't going to tiptoe into this one. "What happened? I feel awful. Did I . . . *assault* that pyr?" Dime's gut wrenched again at the idea. She hadn't meant to do anything. One moment she was walking away and the next moment she was passed out in a car. She hoped no animals had been injured in the fissure.

"Xe assaulted Luja. That's where my certainty ends. We'll talk about it. First, I want to hear what happened in Pito. Just the high points for now; we have more to discuss."

That was right—she hadn't talked to Ella at all since she first stayed with her, since her trip to the Heartland or her meeting with

Ferala. Dime thought about her trip to the forest city, the pyrsi she had met through that one strange night—pyrsi, like Tikinal, she would have liked to have been friends with. Yet, the biggest surprise, and the most comfort, had been seeing someone she knew. "I like it there, but I don't feel like a Fo-ror. I know I'm not only a Ja-lal anymore, but learning some aspect of my past can't fundamentally change the pyr I've become. It was hard for me to get past that."

Ella sat, thinking. "Suzanne and I, maybe that's why we stayed away, in our secluded little tower. She was a Fo-ror, and always would be. Living among unwelcoming Ja-lal would have felt like a betrayal of that for her, yet she refused to return to the forest, for reasons we've discussed. Me, I was still a Ja-lal. But I was more, with Suzanne at my side. Without a world to accept who we were, we made our own." Ella stared away a moment.

"Now, this is lovely," she said, turning back, "but you need to tell me what happened. The suspense."

Dime half-laughed, half-sighed. "So, I found Ferala."

"I can see that." Ella pointed to the gold-set bottle, poking from her clothing like it was sitting in a big chiller bucket made of fabric.

"It appears there are not just factions, but factions within factions." Dime remembered what Rock had said about Dawn's Circle, also. She pushed back a pang of sadness about leaving Rock there, waiting. "Do you know about a disease that spread through the Heartland? They called it the curse?"

"I heard of it at the Crossing once. Maybe twenty cycles ago?" She stopped, recognizing the connection.

"Yes, they say it was horrible; many Fo-ror died. Most affected were ba'pyrsi. The Fo-ror blamed the Ja-lal for it, one way or another, or maybe it was just a reason to cope with something too cruel to be by chance. Whatever parents I had were told I had died also. In reality, my wings were removed and I was flown here by one of the Seats. He left me in the complex, where Da-da found me."

She didn't really want to say more, and that was the gist

of it anyway. Ella would fill in the blanks. "They called it Project Diamondsong," she added.

Ella flinched. "I procured an old notebook once, about the Great War. It's in my tower, hidden. They used project names for battle strategies, then; they wrote them in stylized titling, like,"—she scribbled on a paper—**DIAMONDSONG**. "This Seat, he was harkening back to those turns."

Dime didn't know what to say about that. It was no more horrible with symbolism attached, though . . . more sinister.

"We need to talk about diamonds." From her tone, Dime was sure she meant the crystals, not the victims. Ella hadn't asked how many ba'pyrsi were treated this way; it was unlike a journalist not to ask. Except, they were here as friends. Dime appreciated that.

Dime became conscious of the diamond around her neck, the one her father had given her. Or, she realized, the one that probably had been placed around her neck. The question was, did Neimano give her the diamond? He'd seemed so fixated on it, seeing her. If Neimano hadn't given her the pendant, then was it hidden when he delivered her?

"Diamonds can be charged with valence," Ella began. "I didn't want to tell you this before, because Suzanne warned me again and again how dangerous valence could be. Oh, she used it all the time, for chores or even a little fun here and there—but not for things she considered important.

"There are elements she taught me about valence. And maybe I should have told you earlier, but I saw no signs of it and I was scared I might endanger you, especially walking into the heart of Fo-ror life as you did."

Dime grew unsettled at the direction this was going.

"Wings are a structure that grows through the heart and emerges behind. Over time, maybe long stretches of time, the Fo-ror learned to use this additional muscle to propel themselves, to fly amongst the trees of the dense forest. Yet, fundamentally, a fairy's wings are an extension of their heart. Not their heart, but an extension of it.

"Diamonds live at the heart of Ada-ji. There is a structure of diamond crystals that creates unique strength. Memory, Suzanne said. Now, imagine a Fo-ror possessed a diamond not just of ordinary quality, or of a jeweler's design, but a massive uncut, natural crystal. Imagine they kept it hung over their heart, often against their skin, for twenty cycles. Now, imagine during that time, the pyr was living cycles of repression and longing, without wings to naturally channel that valence."

Dime's heart was beating loudly in her chest, but she tried to ignore it, not wanting to miss any piece of Ella's theory.

"Your journey to the cliff. You couldn't have possibly pedaled so far or so fast on your own. Dime, from the little I understand, I can't conceive the amount of charge that stone might hold. You must have channeled it into the pedals, or into the toothcar itself."

Dime's analytical mind was being inundated with new facts and ideas; she was filing through them as quickly as she could, but every word Ella uttered had added to that pile. It would take time to sort. Charged diamonds? Valence?

"I can't control valence. I don't have wings." She didn't believe her own words, for she knew what had happened. But it wasn't *possible*.

Ella leaned in and offered both of her hands. Dime slid her own fingers atop Ella's, allowing Ella to gently grasp them.

"Valence does not come from the wings," Ella whispered. "It comes from the heart. Dime— They took your wings. Did they take your heart?"

It was silent in the little sleeping room. Underground as they were, there were no shadows to dance, no birds to sing. Just Dime, Ella, and the thing she had just said that Dime could not ignore.

Dime felt her heart beating inside her. Where it had beat through happiness, sadness, frustration, fear, even embarrassment. It was still there. Dime was still here.

"No. No, they did not."

Ella nodded, releasing Dime's hands. "Using it the way you did, back there outside of the city, was dangerous. Untrained, powerful, driven by love and protection—I am glad no pyrsi were hurt. They could be, though, if it happens again. The Violence is no less devastating whether rooted in love or fear, and we should avoid it for as long and with as much passion as we can."

"What do I do?" Dime asked, slowly accepting this new truth, for she could not deny it. "Would anyone train me?"

"Some would. My opinion—I wouldn't risk it. Even if you find the right coach, they will be used to younger pyrsi. Pyrsi raised in their culture. Pyrsi with wings, and youth, and not laden with burdens, passion, and love as you are. Pyrsi without that incredible stone you carry. We can't say what effect not having wings has had on your development, either. What pyr could train you?"

Ella shook her head. "I thought about this the whole way here and the whole time since. It might sound extreme, but I think . . . you should go to the caves. The . . . diamond caves."

"What?" Dime had just returned from Pito.

"Not for long, just to set your gears. No, please listen." She waved off Dime's questions. "For you, intentionally using valence for the first time would be like opening a long-sealed pickle jar." Dime side-eyed her, looking for signs of humor, but Ella seemed serious about the analogy. "I can't imagine the pressure you would release. Look at what you did back there, without even meaning to."

Pressure releasing. It had felt like that, except more like pent-up energy than some sort of unknown power. She supposed, though, that's what Ella was saying.

"Now, the diamonds, think of them as having an amplifier for your voice. Without the amplifier, you must shout. With it, you can teach yourself to whisper—and still be heard. Surrounded by diamonds, and opening this long-sealed jar, you could start by whispering, and build up. Learn technique. Control. At your own pace and with the nuances you discover. Just, get the touch of it.

"There is another reason too. I can't say I'm an expert on valence, but I did have a lot of time alone with a fairy, and we could only play so many hands of cards or read so many books."

Not possible, Dime again thought.

"I believe Fo-ror can detect the use of valence, as it resonates with them. It's probably why they kept finding you on your way to the cliff. Since you were using such strong valence to drive the car, you were emanating to them, like a beacon."

Dime clasped her hands—so much came into view with those ideas.

"In the diamond caves," Ella continued, "I mean, I've never been there, but from what is said, being surrounded by diamonds should absorb any amount of valence, at least as long as you're responsible with it. As long as you can sneak in—and you *are* a trained IC agent, correct?—as long as you can sneak in, you should be able to practice without anyone even noticing."

Ella grimaced. "It's risky, Dime, but I had another harmed toothcar ride to think about it. I'm so old, they wouldn't let me pedal, you know. That's discrimination. Though I was glad for it; I despise those things. Anyway, it's a lot of effort for you to go there again, I know, and the whole thing is risky. But seeing what I saw back there, I no longer fear for you. I fear for others if you can't learn who you are. And how to control it. This way is the safest one, as best I can measure it."

The necklace felt cool against Dime's chest. "But, we've joked about this. I'm not a chosen one—why am I special?"

"No, not chosen at all. At least, not in any mystical sense. Being selected by this Seat as you were, that changed your life, but it was only a factor. You could have taken a thousand paths from that moment, all those cycles ago. The path you've taken has brought you here. A pyr who sought education, worked hard, built a wonderful family, and all that time—allowed herself to feel. To yearn. To grieve. To change. If you are powerful now, it is because of your choices. No one else's."

"And this," Dime added, lifting out her diamond. "Because of this." Ella couldn't give Dime credit for outside factors. It wasn't so simple.

Ella sighed, her usual tone returning. "Well, I was trying to give you a pep talk. I'm sure the huge diamond helped. So, you were given a boost. What will you do with it?"

Dime didn't answer, knowing it was a question she would need to ask herself.

"Ella, thank you for all this. As always, you're a great friend."

Ella shook a finger. "I don't think twice counts as always. But I'll take it. Thanks. Now, this has been the real deal and I love your accommodations, but I don't want to start any rumors of my living alone here with your lovely spouse, so I'd best be getting back."

Dime knew Ella didn't like leaving her large indoor plant, Friend, for long. She still wondered what type of plant Friend was, as it was not familiar to her. She considered asking, but Ella seemed emotional enough.

"I want to make sure Juni didn't head back to my tower, or if she did, I'll find her there. Newts are wonderful, but they will *wreck* your garden. Of course, if I hear anything about your child, I'll send word. And I'll spend some time in the city. See if I can't keep truth to the rumors. A journalist's best brand of valence." She winked.

"Ella?" Dime had one more question. "I have an image of my mind, of you murmuring. Before I ... before the fissure. I was worried whether you were alright."

Ella's shoulders drooped. "It was an idea I had, perhaps to say I really was the old witch, and maybe that would scare them off."

Dime nodded slowly, understanding. It was like the decision she'd made when she'd entered the city, and she'd regretted it ever since. "I'm so glad that you didn't. Whatever happened." She tried to think how to verbalize what she was thinking. "Who we are should never be compromised to placate those who see us differently." Their eyes met for a long stride, and Ella nodded.

She had the feeling Ella thought Dime was missing something. Dime almost asked her, but Ella was never shy about speaking, and she'd already stood to leave.

They walked out to the common area together. Luja was reading vis book, and Dayn was aimlessly stirring a cup of brew. The spoon clattered to the side when they walked in.

"Ella needs to head back. Maybe she'll drink to us when she gets there." She threw her a knowing grin and Ella rolled her eyes.

"It's my gift, isn't it? Sol's goodness."

"Will you be alright—without a car, I mean?"

"Stop it. I don't mind the walk, anyway. Keeps me strong." She flexed an arm muscle, though under her baggy tunic there wasn't much effect.

"Oh, one thing—maybe I should give you this, for when you're in the city." Dime hopped into her room, took the compass from her bag, and returned with it.

"I meant to get this looked at in Lodon. Maybe you can take it back and— *Hmm.* See, now this is different. It's pointing sur, but it's jumpy again. It works fine in Lodon, but when I was in the Beds, it pointed what I knew from Sha to be eas, not sur. And in Pito, it jumped all over the place."

Ella held a hand up, like she was thinking. She lowered it. "I've never had one, myself, but . . . maybe they point toward the diamonds. Toward the caves."

Dime closed her eyes and reached for her pendant, which still hung over her shirt. "It does. I'm certain. Don't ask me how I know; I just do. Kind of silly I didn't realize it, I guess." She clipped the little wristband on. "My Circlemates had no idea." Dime smiled.

"Oh, I'm sure they didn't. So many of our instincts come from forces we don't understand. That's why I say, trust your gut."

"Even when your gut lands you in a bucket of pickles?"

Ella grinned. "Sometimes especially. Now, behave yourself. Or don't. Stop in anytime. Ok?"

"Of course." Dime reached forward, and Ella accepted her hug. Luja and Dayn offered theirs as well. Dime figured they'd all been through a lot together. It didn't always take time to form a bond.

"You take care of your Ma-ma." Ella pointed at Luja.

"I will." Luja responded like a medic taking orders. Dime smiled.

"Dayn, you're a lucky ma'pyr."

He laughed, fairly heartily. "I sure am." He grinned at Ella, who winked back. Dime had no idea what they were going on about, but she was glad to see them smiling.

There were no further words as Ella turned and walked up the long staircase—and was gone.

They sat for a while, each lost in thought. "Turns out, there's more," Dime began, breaking the silence. As outrageous as her suggestion seemed, Dime was going to trust Ella. It solved a second problem, too. "With your permission, I have somewhere I think I should go. Just for a short trip. I'm sorry; I know I just got back."

She was surprised that neither looked upset, though not exactly happy either. Dime wasn't ready to tell them she might be able to control valence, though they probably already knew. That goal felt almost secondary to the other, one she'd worried she couldn't solve for a while, but given an opportunity, she was sure going to try.

"Do you remember the IC agent who snooped on you after . . . the incident? Asked about me?"

Dayn tapped his lip. "Oh, Agent Rock? She's a friend, right? I had the sense I could trust her." He looked like he had more to say, but his words trailed off.

"Yeah, her. We go way back. And you can trust her. At least, I plan to." Dime paused. "She's being held against her will, well sort of, in Pito. In addition to what I think I need to do there, I can also get her out. I wouldn't have gone back so soon, but if I'm going, then I can help her." Dime felt good about that; it helped with her decision. She was still working through the valence piece, anyway.

Dayn leaned back. "I need to stay here—not that I heard an invitation to go with you—but I'll stay here with Luja and also because this is where Tum knows to find us."

"If she doesn't come back," Dime said, hoping to reassure him, "I know where to find her. It's not close, but we could get there. Until then, I trust that she's well."

He nodded. Clearly the uncertainty of their youngest being away was weighing on him. Perhaps it should weigh more on Dime as well, but it felt like one of many burdens now, and a lesser one, for at least Tum was in very capable . . . arms. She knew Dayn would not leave here until Tum had returned, not if there were any chance she was on her way, trying to find this den. And now, Dime was adding another weight by leaving so soon.

Watching their pensive gazes, she couldn't leave it at this. Tired of knots in her throat and secrets and revelations and embarrassment, she just made herself say it. "I'm going to try and learn valence. In the caves, where it will be safer for me to experiment. That's the thing I was just saying."

"Well, you are a fairy, Ma-ma," Luja said with a grin. "Maybe Tum was right about that. It would be . . . awesome."

Dime looked at Luja, still giggling, unaware of Dayn's warm gaze, drawing warmth from vis laughter. She imagined Tum and Juni playing in the forest, with Tum designing carriers to bring back food, or carving vessels to catch the rain. She pictured Da-da, back in his home, writing stories and belting fantastical tunes. Ador and Batu, seeking the latest rumors. And Zael, facing death with life in his eyes. She remembered Rock, waiting in the stark, lonely cage, having given Dime her only way out. She thought of Ella, and Suzanne, gone but never apart.

Did they take her heart?

No. And they never would.

End of Part 03

About the Author

E.D.E. Bell was born in the year of the fire dragon during a Cleveland blizzard. After a youth in the mitten, an MSE in Electrical Engineering from the University of Michigan, three wonderful children, and nearly two decades in Northern Virginia and Southwest Ohio developing technical intelligence strategy, she now applies her magic to the creation of genre-bending fantasy fiction in Ferndale, Michigan, where she is proud to be part of the Detroit arts community. A passionate vegan and enthusiastic denier of gender rules, she feels strongly about issues related to human equality and animal compassion. She revels in garlic. She loves cats and trees. You can follow her adventures at edebell.com.

Continue Dime's story in . . .

Part 04: Magic

edebell.com/diamondsong

www.ingramcontent.com/pod-product-compliance
Lightning Source LLC
Chambersburg PA
CBHW032037180726

48284CB00008B/2626